WHERE IS GOD

A Question Everyone Should Ask

— by —

VINAL PIERS

Table of Contents

Foreword

Just as this book was to be submitted for publication, I received a message from a couple I went to church with. His wife said I was one of five people she had committed to pray for this year. I told her I was about to publish a book and wanted God to use it in reaching others. Intercession is so crucial yet so overlooked. Her prayer blew me away. I was both humbled and honored by it. This is the prayer she sent.

Heavenly Father,

Thank You for the faithfulness You have shown Vinal over these 45 years. Thank You for every testimony, every valley, every miracle, and even the chapters written through tears. What a gift that he has captured these stories so others can see that You are steady, present, and good.

Lord, we especially honor the chapter born from the loss of his son. You see that pain. You saw it then, and You still see it. Thank You for redeeming what was so devastating and for using his obedience and faith to soften another grieving mother's heart. Only You can bring that kind of beauty from ashes. Thank You for the woman who forgave, who received You, and who was given eight more years of life. What mercy. What grace.

As this book prepares to be released on Amazon, go before it. Guide it into the hands of the people who need it most, the grieving, the questioning, the ones wondering how to forgive, how to trust, how to keep going. Let his words carry Your presence. Let every testimony point clearly to Your faithfulness.

Protect Vinal's heart as these stories go public. Cover him with peace. Heal any places that still ache. Fill him with joy as he sees the fruit of decades of walking with You.

May this book not simply be read but may it minister. May it open hearts, restore hope, and lead many to salvation.

IN JESUS' POWERFUL AND FAITHFUL NAME, AMEN

AMY DORMAN

Preface

I'm writing this book for several reasons. My hope and prayer is that readers can relate to the struggles they have faced in their own lives. Believer, unbeliever, and those who are undecided. It's dedicated to my wife and children for listening to these stories countless times. This memoir includes several poems I've written that were inspired by different events. Situations and circumstances in your life will be different. Allow God to create a solution just for you. He's very creative. He doesn't even make two snowflakes identical. People like formulas, we don't know what we like; we like what we know.

I really don't consider myself a religious person. I'm just a sinner saved by grace, for which I'm eternally thankful. Twice in my life, I have been denied communion because I didn't know that particular church's protocol. One woman actually came to the back of the church where I was seated and took the sacraments away from me. I guess it was obvious. I just smiled when she took them from me. I'm not easily offended, but I easily offend. Throughout this book, I use the term 'I prayed.' Prayer doesn't have to be a time set aside, done in a church, or kneeling at the side of your bed. It's simply talking to God. If you are a Christian, it should be your initial response to a situation. Reactions usually have consequences. This book won't contain a lot of filler material, just condensed stories of actual events that have happened in my life. All I ask is that you read them with an open mind/spirit.

As I'm writing, I've noticed a pattern where I repeatedly only encounter a person once and never see them again. Maybe that's why we should make the most of every opportunity. It may be the only interaction we'll ever have with that person. Ricky Texada, a dear pastor friend, taught me that when someone asks you for prayer, you should pray with them right then, as we tend to forget. When I share testimonies with people of what God did in my life, many have said, "I want God to do that in my life," or "How did you make that happen?" As if there's some 'God button' they can push. I understand what they're saying, but that's not what made it happen. Any preconceived ideas you may have of how or what He will do in your circumstances need to be set aside. *"For now, we see only a reflection as in a mirror; then we shall see face to face. Now I know in part; then I shall know fully, even as I am fully known." 1 Corinthians 13:12 NIV* Jesus himself prayed,

"O My Father, if it is possible, let this cup pass from Me; nevertheless, not as I will, but as You will." Matthew 26:39 NKJV He created each of us as individuals and will custom-design a personal solution tailored to your circumstances. Always ask God to give you peace when you pray regarding a matter, and go with your peace. If you don't have peace, you'll only have pieces.

I had an employee say to me once, "Every time you tell a story, it's exactly the same, down to the smallest detail. It never changes." I smiled and said, "At least you know I'm telling the truth." Throughout this book, I refer to God speaking to me. I don't ever recall hearing an audible voice, just that He speaks in a still small voice. 1 Kings 19:12 NKJV

MY Prayer God Help

I was driving my Mustang down Belmont St in Brockton, Massachusetts, in late spring of 1979, having no clear direction as to where I was headed in life. I was studying Law Enforcement in college and had been told that because I was blind in my left eye due to a recent BB gun accident, my hopes of a career in Law Enforcement were slim to none. I then tried joining the military, but they PDQ'd me, (permanently disqualified) due to my blindness. Had I joined, I never would have met my wife.

The Bible says, ***"We know that God causes everything to work together for the good of those who love God and are called according to his purpose for them." Romans 8:28 NLT***

Life without direction or a sense of purpose is a dangerous place to be. It can easily lead you on a downhill path of hopelessness. I watched an experiment on hypothermia where a person was lowered into frigid water to study the effects it has on people. They had thermometers on his extremities and also his core. After some time, the temperature of his extremities dropped significantly so he couldn't feel his arms or legs. His core temperature maintained 98.6 degrees. He said he was coherent and as long as he was able to float he thought he'd be fine. His body was in survival mode and focused on maintaining his core temperature. Some time later, he said, "If I couldn't see a ship or some means of rescue, I'd begin to think I wasn't going to make it." As soon as he said that, his body started shutting down and his core temperature started to drop. They immediately lifted him out of the water ending the experiment. Being without hope is a dangerous place to be. ***"Hope deferred makes the heart grow sick." Proverbs 13:12 NIV.***

If you don't know where you're going, any path will get you there. I remember simply praying, "God help." That was it. No eloquent prayer of some long since departed saint, just two simple words of someone lost and in need of direction. Nothing happened immediately, but that simple prayer set things in motion.

I came across Billy Graham's book 'How to be Born Again.' I don't remember where I got it from. For a majority of the first part of the book, he emphasized repeatedly, "without the shedding of blood there is no forgiveness of sin." I remember thinking I had to buy a chicken or something and cut its head off in the woods somewhere because I'd done some bad things. The blood of something innocent has to be shed to atone for sin.

Setting the Ten Commandments aside, greed, pride, and lust are enough to make anyone a sinner. In the book, he finally explained that Jesus shed his innocent blood for us to cleanse us from all of our sin. All I had to do was accept and receive what He already did for me. I was raised in a Baptist home, and this was a revelation to me? I believed that in my mind, but it had never taken hold in my heart. The revelation of God's grace was just that, a revelation. It was so simple, even too simple. All I needed to do was accept His forgiveness as a free gift. I couldn't earn it by trying to be good enough, going to church, or striving to do the right thing through some penance.

If we could attain it in and of ourselves, Jesus wouldn't have had to die in our place. Grace is unmerited favor. We don't deserve it, and can't earn it. It's a free gift. I was free!

I was also very relieved that I didn't have to go kill some poor chicken.

I gave the book to Carol and told her she had to read it. We weren't dating at the time, and she really wasn't interested. She thought the book was some New Age thing.

She had never heard the phrase "born again" until she read an article in Cosmopolitan magazine about people having a ceremony and a rebirth experience in a bathtub. Although she took the book from me, she thought I had lost my mind if I thought she was going to get naked in a bathtub in a room full of people and experience rebirth. She planned to only read a few pages, then give it back to me. She started reading it that night and quickly learned the born-again experience Billy Graham explained was nothing like what she had read in Cosmopolitan magazine.

She couldn't put the book down. She read the entire book that night and discovered the wonder of God's love, forgiveness, and grace.

A week or so later, my brother-in-law asked me if I wanted to work with him at a restaurant he wanted to buy. He said he couldn't pay me anything, but if it was successful, we would be equal partners (sweat equity). I wasn't the least bit excited about working eighty plus hours per week without pay, but I knew I couldn't keep partying because that lifestyle led nowhere. Due to the hours involved, I wouldn't have time for anything else. I now had a vision and a future goal.

We had the store for a couple of months when my brother-in-law told me we were going to have to give the store back to the seller because it wasn't making any money. I was terrified and immediately went into the backroom to pray. I told God He needed to do something. My prayer was simply along the lines of, God, you put me here for a reason, and it wasn't to fail. If we were to fail, I knew I'd probably fall back into the partying lifestyle. That night, something happened. I remember it was a Wednesday, and we were three times busier than we'd ever been. The business took off from that point. Within six months, sales had increased by fifty percent. Sales were averaging four hundred and twenty-five percent higher by the time my brother-in-law bought me out in 1985, when Carol and I moved to Texas.

Twenty and Clueless

Carol and I dated when we were in college. Since we were so young, we got scared at the strength of our feelings for each other, and we broke up several times. I told a friend of mine that she was the kind of girl you marry. After we dedicated our lives to Christ, I started pursuing Carol again. She didn't want to date me, but prayed about it. Since she had prayed and received an answer from God, she was devastated when I broke our engagement. She knew what God had said, and this wasn't part of that picture. What crushed her most was that she believed what God had told her, not that I broke our engagement. She wouldn't have started dating me again if God hadn't told her this relationship was His will for her life.

I was a real self-centered, double minded jerk and didn't deserve her. I broke our engagement in March 1980. Carol moved back to California to get as far away from me as she could. I begged her not to leave, but the damage was done. Her heart toward me was like stone. Failure to make decisions (or lack thereof) results in decisions being made for you. When Carol decided to leave, I tried to convince myself it was the best thing for us. This way, we couldn't just start seeing each other again as we had done countless times in our two-year dating history. A week after she left, in April 1980, the song "She's out of my life" by Michael Jackson was released. I was never a Michael Jackson fan, but the song nailed exactly where I was at.

These are the lyrics:

"She's out of my life... She's out of my life...

And I don't know whether to laugh or cry

I don't know whether to live or die, and it cuts like a knife

She's out of my life.... It's out of my hands......It's out of my hands....

To think that for two years, she was here, and I took her for granted. I was so cavalier.

Now the way that it stands..... she's out of my hands

So I've learned that love's not possession, and I've learned that love won't wait

Now I've learned that love needs expression, but I learned too late

She's out of my life.... She's out of my life.

Damned indecision and cursed pride, kept my love for her locked deep inside.

And it cuts like a knife...... She's out of my life."

We had even dated for two years. "She's Out of My Life" by Michael Jackson was on the Billboard Hot 100 Chart for seventeen weeks. It peaked at top ten songs during the week of April 10, 1980. Everywhere I went, the song would play and remind me of how I screwed up. Even a popular song can draw us back to God's plan and destiny.

Our youngest daughter asked me once (it was actually on April 19, 2014) if Mom and I had a song. I said, "She's out of my Life" She laughed and said, "What?" I explained it to her.

God once again redeemed our relationship and healed the wounds and bound up the broken hearted. We erect walls as a defence mechanism and a means of self-preservation because we don't want to be hurt again. God can break down the walls we build. He wants to, but respects our free will and needs us to let Him. Ask God what your part in that is.

This year, we'll celebrate forty-six years of marriage.

He alone knows the end from the beginning. I was twenty-one, and she had just turned twenty when we were married. Because we were so young, I jokingly tell people the only baggage we brought into our marriage was carry-on

Where is God?

Events will happen to each one of us in life that we have no control over. Some of them are things we weren't even responsible for. It could be a diagnosis, an accident, or a phone call in the middle of the night. Some things we have no advance warning of. They hit us like a freight train. What we are oblivious to, are things God didn't allow to happen in our lives.

An example in my life was holding the lifeless body of our son. I just kept asking God why. It made no sense. He was perfect. When we're confronted with circumstances or situations that can and do overwhelm us, or potentially cause us to overreact, we need to *"Take heed, and be quiet; do not fear or be fainthearted." Isaiah 7:4 NKJV*.

Twice in the book of Jeremiah chapter 2, God says, *"My people did not ask where is the Lord."* The first time God directed it at His people, the second time it was directed at the priests. In the book of Job (pronounced Jobe), Job says, *"I cry out to you, God, but you do not answer" Job 30:20 NIV*

There are times we can all relate to this Psalm: *"Awake, Lord! Why do you sleep? Rouse yourself! Do not reject us forever. Why do you hide your face and forget our misery and oppression? We are brought down to the dust; our bodies cling to the ground. Rise up and help us; rescue us because of your unfailing love." Psalm 44:23-26 NIV* God doesn't have a problem with us questioning Him. He actually expects it.

As with any relationship, you're bound to have disagreements. God is no exception. What we need to guard ourselves from is hardening our hearts towards Him. In the Book of Job, God asks *Job, "Would you condemn Me to justify yourself?" Job 40:8 NIV.* I have meditated on that verse countless times in my life when questioning God. Job's own wife told him to "curse God and die." It is an option we have, but it's the worst decision we could make.

In the Book of Judges, Gideon asked the angel of the Lord, *"If the LORD is with us, why has all this happened to us? Where are all the wonders that our ancestors told us about when they said, 'Did not the LORD bring us up out of Egypt?' But now the LORD has abandoned us and given us into the hand of Midian." Judges 6:13 NIV.*

Without a doubt, God will allow us to face things that can and do overwhelm us. He will ABSOLUTELY let us go through things we can't handle on our own. What God won't allow is for us to be tempted beyond what we can bear, but will provide us with a way out. *"The temptations in your life are no different from what others experience. And God is faithful. He will not allow the temptation to be more than you can stand. When you are tempted, he will show you a way out so that you can endure." 1 Corinthians 10:13 NLT* Temptation isn't sin by the way. It's what you do with the temptation. Even Jesus was tempted. *"But each one is tempted, when he is drawn away by his own lust, and enticed. Then, when desire has conceived, it gives birth to sin; and sin, when it is full-grown, brings forth death." James 1:14,15 NKJV*

A pastor friend said that he was thankful that opportunity and weakness never crossed the same path he was on. At a time of weakness, there was no opportunity. We must *"Let perseverance finish its work so that you may be mature and complete, not lacking anything." James 1:4 NIV* Allowing perseverance to finish its work is a choice.

In John 10:27, Jesus said, his sheep listen to his voice: I know them, and they follow me, and they won't follow the voice of a stranger. Jesus also said, everything should be established by the testimony of two or three witnesses. I'm a firm believer in God confirming something to you.

A good friend of mine owned a few dozen Domino pizza locations. He came into our store one day, and I asked him if he had picked his new area supervisor yet. He said no and that he'd been putting it off because he didn't want the person he didn't promote to be hurt by his decision. I said, "Why don't you pray and ask God who He wants you to put in that position and ask Him for a confirmation?" "He'll do that?" He asked? I smiled and said, of course. That way, you can remind Him it was His decision should any problems arise from it in the future. He was shocked that God would be that involved in his business. A couple of weeks later, he came back in and told me God had told him who to promote and gave him his confirmation two days later. He said, "Do you know how many people I've shared that with?" Each one of us needs to know what God has said and stand on that. In the Garden of Eden, that was the question that led to the fall. ***"Did God really say?" Genesis 3:1.*** After Jesus had fasted for forty days in the desert, Satan came and tempted Him. Notice Satan waited to tempt Him until he was in his weakest physical state. How did Jesus respond? He quoted scripture. Satan also knows scripture and will use it out of context.

"The devil said to him, 'If you are the Son of God, tell this stone to become bread." Jesus answered, "It is written: 'Man shall not live on bread alone." The devil led him up to a high place and showed him in an instant all the kingdoms of the world. And he said to him, "I will give you all their authority and splendor; it has been given to me, and I can give it to anyone I want to. (I find it interesting that Jesus didn't correct him and say they weren't his to give.) You've probably heard of people who have said they sold their souls to the devil for fame and fortune. *'If you worship me, it will all be yours." Jesus answered, "It is written: 'Worship the Lord your God and serve him only." The devil led him to Jerusalem and had him stand on the highest point*

of the temple. "If you are the Son of God," he said, "throw yourself down from here. For it is written: "'He will command his angels concerning you to guard you carefully; they will lift you up in their hands, so that you will not strike your foot against a stone. (Psalm 91) Jesus answered, "It is said: 'Do not put the Lord your God to the test."

When the devil had finished all this tempting, he left him until an opportune time." Luke 4:3-13 NIV

As you will read, God even cares about the smallest details in our lives. It is written, ***"What is man that you are mindful of them, Or the son of man that you take care of him?" Hebrews 2:6 NIV*** and ***"Lord, what is man, that You take knowledge of him? Or the son of man, that You are mindful of him?" Psalms 144:3 NKJV***

We are the apple of His eye. I've often wondered why He didn't just let Adam and Eve die when they sinned and start over. He didn't because He's committed to what He starts. God hasn't abandoned you.

We all go through times of pruning. Just remember, the gardener is closest to the vine during the pruning process. Without tests, we won't have testimonies.

At our first restaurant, an employee named Joe asked me for advice regarding his finances. I asked him how much he earned the previous week. He laughed and said, Sixty-eight dollars and change. My brother-in-law wanted him to quit, so he wasn't giving him many hours. To keep things in perspective, minimum wage was $3.35 an hour, and his rent was fifty dollars a week. I told him to set aside seven dollars for his tithe. The tithe belongs to God. A tithe is ten percent of whatever you make. He laughed and said he only had fourteen dollars left. I said, "I don't care if you only have seven." God doesn't need your money, He wants you to trust Him. After an hour or so of discussion, he agreed to set it aside.

Within a day or two, my brother-in-law's favorite employee quit and walked out. Joe got all of his hours in addition to his own. A couple of months later, Joe came up to me and said he had over four hundred and fifty dollars set aside in his tithe. I said, "Boy, that seven dollars seems pretty insignificant now, doesn't it?" He said, "Tell me about it."

After we moved to Texas, Joe started borrowing from his tithe to buy things. He told me he was keeping a running total. I don't know if he ever got caught up. I later learned that he and a friend stole a motorhome and got arrested. I lost track of Joe after that. Joe never claimed to be a Christian, but learned firsthand what God can and will do if you trust Him. Joe will never forget, nor can he deny what God did for him.

God actually tells us to 'test Him' regarding the tithe. *"Test me in this," says the LORD Almighty, "and see if I will not throw open the floodgates of heaven and pour out so much blessing that there will not be room enough to store it," Malachi 3:10 NIV.*

Joe didn't give his tithe to any organization or church, he had simply set it aside in his dresser.

My children have heard these stories countless times and have said to me, "Dad, you've told me this story before." I just smile and say things like, "Humor me, I'll probably tell you a few more times before I die, and you're going to miss hearing them when I'm gone." They don't like it when I say that, but it's true. My experiences with God are just that, they're mine. It's what He did for me. My experiences won't be enough to sustain my children's walk in life. They all need their own. God has no grandchildren, only children. What can be shaken, will be shaken. I remember asking my dad when I was around ten if grandpa had ever told him the same story twice. (My grandfather was a lumberjack, born in Northern Maine in 1900, and had a lot of stories.) My dad laughed and said, "He's told me the story of the bear they called three toes dozens of times." Why don't you tell him you've already heard it I asked? He said because he loves telling them, I enjoy hearing them, and it's a way I can honor him.

Like it or not, we all go through things in life that will impact and shape us into who we become. We must not allow even the most extreme circumstances to spiritually cripple us. We will either become better through them or embittered by them. God has placed spiritual gold 'if you will' inside each and every one of us. A very small percentage of that gold is in nugget form and easy to spot. Everyone loves nuggets (our gifts and abilities) Nuggets simply reveal where the gold is. The bulk of the gold is in tiny specs hidden among tons of ore. The ore has to first be crushed, then processed through multiple steps in order to extract the gold.

'The stone which the builders rejected Has become the chief cornerstone' "Whoever falls on that stone will be broken; but on whomever it falls, it will grind him to powder." Luke 20:17,18 NKJV

Finally, gold is purified by fire. As it heats up, the remaining impurities rise to the surface and the dross is removed. We determine the level of processing we allow God to do in our lives. We also determine the intensity of the fire and the duration of the flame. It is written, *"For by one sacrifice he has made perfect forever those who are <u>being made holy.</u>" Hebrews 1;13 NIV*

We also have the ability to shut the process down. Our refining isn't fun, but it's crucial in determining who we ultimately become. Jesus said, *"I counsel you to buy from me gold refined in the fire, so you can become rich" Revelation 3:18 NIV.*

God will use the circumstances you overcame in life to reach someone going through a similar situation that may have shut the door to their heart towards Him decades ago.

"For we are God's handiwork, created in Christ Jesus to do good works, which God prepared in advance for us to do." Ephesians 2:10 NIV. Have you ever heard someone say, "I'm still here, God must have something He still wants me to do?"

Our relationship with Him needs to be as transparent as it can be. He knows everything anyway. He loves us in spite of ourselves. He loves us to the point that He chose to send His only begotten Son to die as the sacrificial lamb in our place to make atonement for our sins. Yet we resist and think we can somehow hide from Him. *"Where can I go from your Spirit? Where can I flee from your presence? If I go up to the heavens, you are there; if I make my bed in the depths, you are there." Psalm 139:7,8 NIV.* He's the Alpha and Omega. The beginning and the end.

The Moon is Not the Son

In the first few months we had our first restaurant, a young man named Philipe with the Unification Church came into our restaurant selling peanut brittle for three dollars. He told me he was a Christian missionary, so I gave him the twenty dollars I had and told him to keep the change. I figured since he was a 'missionary', he would have more need for it than I would. He invited me to come to the house they had rented as their base in Brockton. Everyone told me to stay away from them because they were a cult. When I asked why they were considered a cult, no one could tell me, which I didn't think was fair so I read some of their background history.

Unification Church members were commonly called moonies back then. Their leader was Sun Myung Moon from Korea. The night Carol and I went to their house, there were six to eight other people there, whom they had evangelized while street witnessing. People just want to be loved. They will respond when someone reaches out to them and shows them some compassion. There was a huge Scofield Reference Bible on the table next to me. I opened it up and saw a picture of Sun Myung Moon. I held it up and said, "Who's this guy?" I knew who he was when I asked. It made them noticeably uncomfortable. They reverently bowed their heads and said, "That's our founding father." I thought, "Oh, that hit a nerve." I was sceptical of them but thought I should at least hear what they had to say. The missionaries from the Unification Church ultimately told me it was ok to lie for the glory of the Lord. I knew that was wrong, and it helped me to learn the difference between their church and true Christianity. If someone won't come to the Lord through truth, they won't come. God respects our freedom of choice. The Father wants disciples, not converts. When the majority of Jesus' disciples "turned and followed Him no more" because His teachings were too hard, He let them leave. Interestingly, that passage in the Bible is John 6:66. Jesus then turned to the twelve and asked if they wanted to leave also. Peter replied, **"Lord, to whom shall we go? You have the words of eternal life." John 6:68 NIV.**

Philipe kept insisting I go to their retreat compound in upstate NY. I finally agreed to go under the condition that he visit my church first. He agreed. My church at the time was the Brockton Assembly of God on Warren Ave. Several weeks later, when Philipe showed up, the church was packed. Philipe came in towards the end of the worship songs. He sang, clapped, and even raised his hands. No one knew he was coming. I didn't even know he was coming. Towards the end of the service, there was a message in tongues (Book of Acts chapter two) from the other side of the church, followed by the interpretation. The interpretation was along these lines: *There is someone in here trying to deceive my children. Why are you resisting me? Soften your heart, and I will forgive you also.* I knew exactly who that word was for! Philipe had a terrified look on his face.

The service ended a few minutes later, and I asked him what he thought. He said it was very interesting, but he needed to leave. He literally ran out of the church, and I never saw him again. I never did go on their retreat.

A month or so later, a guy named Stephen, who was at the 'Moonie' house that night saw me in a parking lot in downtown Brockton. He recognized me from that night and ran up to me as I was getting in my car. I asked him to get in my car because it was freezing outside. He said there was something about them he didn't trust, but he felt he could trust me. I explained the Gospel to him and led him in a sinner's prayer in the parking lot. I tried to find him for weeks afterwards to follow up with him, but never saw him again.

New Beginnings in Texas

Carol and I moved to Texas in 1985 to open a restaurant called Sub-Conscious. We wanted to introduce east coast style subs to Texas and never look back. We also wanted God to pick our location. Our goal was to serve great food with an eternal purpose. We prayed and fasted as to where He wanted us to open and had narrowed it down to two locations. One location was in a new plaza that had never been finished out. If we chose that spot, we could custom-design it to our needs. The other location was in an older plaza that was directly across the street from the high school. It had already been finished out, so we would have to make the existing dimensions work.

We were undecided as to which location God wanted us in. We drove out to Last Days Ministries in Lindale, Texas, to clear our thoughts. It felt like we were stuck, facing a giant wall in front of us. Last Days was founded by the late Keith Green and his wife, Melody. We had supported their ministry since 1979. If you're not familiar with Keith Green, I highly recommend listening to his No Compromise story and music on YouTube. Carol and I had both felt called to the mission field for years. As a young married couple in 1981/82, we tried to move to Last Days, but they told us no. They were only set up for singles at the time. We had plenty of money and hadn't committed a dime towards the restaurant. Do we pursue our own goals, or His call? We were at a crucial point in our Christian walk and told God, "Not our will but your will be done."

We got home from Last Days and believed God wanted us to open our store and wanted it to be our mission field. We were still undecided on its location. I really wanted the spot in the new plaza, but felt like God wanted us in the location across from the high school. I asked God for a fleece. A fleece is a sign or confirmation when seeking God. Gideon asked God for one in the Old Testament and then asked for a second one as confirmation. *Book of Judges 6:37-40.*

We had a Bunny Ears cactus we'd had for several years that was over five feet tall. Above the three-foot height, nothing had grown out of the sides, only straight up. I said, Ok God, if you want us to go in across from the high school, I want a growth to come out of the side of that cactus tomorrow above the three-foot mark. You can do that if that's where you really want us to go. The next day, I went outside and saw a tiny bud coming out of the side. I was shocked but not totally convinced. I thought that was going to come out anyway. I told God I want another one to come out by tomorrow. I REALLY didn't want to go across from the high school. The next morning, there was a second bud on the opposite side. God would later use my bold (even arrogant) confirmation request. When I told the commercial real estate group I was taking the other location, they offered me ridiculous concessions to change my mind. Having just read the story of what almost happened to Balaam when he changed his mind because he was offered more money (The Book of Numbers chapter 22), I wasn't about to change mine. I knew beyond a shadow of doubt exactly where God wanted me.

The following poem is based on that time in our lives.

HEAR THE CALL

When I first came to know the Lord, my heart was set on fire

To seek His ways and know His truths, it was my heart desire

Early in this newfound walk, I felt a mission call

Those of which I dismissed, that's not for me at all

The pioneer inside of me, sang a different song

As far as what God planned for me, I'd just bring Him along

Until one day, my plans and dreams all suddenly seemed to stop

In front of me He'd placed a wall, and I couldn't climb its top

He told me that His plan for me, was of His own design

And of my future hopes and dreams, of these I must resign

No longer could I brush Him off, and just forsake His call

He told me that if I do this, then He's not Lord of all

I told Him that I knew this so, His will I said I'd live

He told me once I'd crossed that line, my son you I forgive

Now set free from my own dreams, I sought the mission's call

I then realized, to my surprise, t'was not His will at all

This was you see, a test for me, would I drop all I'd planned

If He should choose to send me to, some distant foreign land

If God's been dealing with your heart, please don't forsake His call

The very thing you think He wants, He may not want at all ©

Pregnant With Our First-Born

When Carol became pregnant with our first child, our restaurant was thriving and we'd been open for two years. I was terrified. What did I know about being a father? I didn't want to screw this child's head up by doing something wrong. I was bound to make mistakes. I also knew I was highly likely to make the same mistakes my father did. Deep down, I knew I had one shot at raising this child, and I was terrified. I prayed fervently and told God that He would have to teach me to be a great dad.

A couple of months before her due date, Carol went to a small women's gathering with my sister. Before they left, a woman there asked Carol if she could pray for her baby, which Carol agreed to. When she was praying, she said, this baby is very anointed. He will go to the ends of the earth preaching the Gospel. When I got home that night, Carol told me what the woman had prayed. I said, he? She said he? So we're having a boy? We hadn't had a sonogram because we wanted it to be a surprise. Deep down, I wanted our first born to be a son. I had told Carol that if we had a boy, we were naming him Vinal. She said, "What if he's not an extrovert like you? He may resent it?" There was no telling me otherwise. If it's a boy, we're naming him Vinal.

A few weeks later, we received a newsletter in the mail from a church in Dallas. Inside was the story about Joshua, Achan, and the Battle of Jericho (Joshua chapter 7). Carol read it while I was at work. She said, Joshua… that's a nice name. She said a quick prayer that if it's a boy and God wanted him to be named Joshua, that I was going to have to suggest it. Praying for God to speak to your spouse is so much more effective and fruitful than addressing it yourself. I got home and saw the newsletter on the kitchen table and read the story. I went into the living room and asked her if she had read the story in the newsletter. She looked at me and said, "What do you mean?" I said, "Did you read it?" She said yes but didn't want to tell me what she'd prayed. I asked her what she got out of it. She thought about it and said, "Joshua was a very obedient servant of the Lord." Immediately, I thought of what that woman had said about him going to the ends of the earth preaching the Gospel. I thought someone who did that would have to be obedient. I said, "If it's a boy, do you want to name him Joshua?" Her eyes filled with tears. I said, "What's the matter?" It was then she told me what she had prayed. I said, "We've got to tell people!" "Tell them what?" she asked. "Tell them we're having a son and God wants us to name him Joshua!" I replied. She said, "You can't tell people that." I said, "Oh no? Watch me."

At first, I told everyone. Not everyone was as excited as I seemed to be. I decided to limit telling the story to only the people who asked if we knew what we were having. Which was usually followed by, oh you had a sonogram. No, God told us. It was then I told them the story. I remember I told one couple that had a martial arts studio the story about his name. They came in the day he was born and asked an employee if we'd had the baby yet. She told them we had it this morning. He said, they had a boy, didn't they? She asked how they knew. He told us they were having a boy and were naming him Joshua.

We will never know the impact we will have on the lives of others we cross paths with. Just because you don't see immediate results, know that you've planted a seed. Seeds can take decades and even centuries for the right conditions to germinate. For the record, our son's middle name is Vinal.

Deliver us from Evil

A much avoided topic among believers is deliverance, yet it was a third of Jesus' ministry. We love His teachings, and most will pray for healing, but very little on deliverance is mentioned, let alone taught. There's a story in the Book of Acts, chapter 19:11-20, where the seven sons of Sceva tried their hand at deliverance after witnessing it happening through believers. They would say, "In the name of Jesus whom Paul preaches," we command you to come out. One day, a spirit answered them and said, "Jesus I know, and I know about Paul, but who are you?" It says the possessed man overpowered them all, and they ran out of the house naked and bleeding.

When Jesus told the Disciples He was giving them authority over "snakes and scorpions" Luke 10:19. It could have been Him differentiating between the types of spirits and that certain ones only come out by "prayer and fasting." Some translations of the New Testament omit the word fasting, but I believe it is crucial in some cases. I'll explain a little later.

In mid November 1987, I had been fasting for three days, asking God to use me. There was a twenty-year-old woman who worked lunch for us along with two others. God told me to ask her if I could pray for her. It was kind of awkward due to the other two employees who were there. They all left together, and I felt awful for not asking her.

I went into the back, prayed, and repented for not asking her. I said, I'm sorry, Lord. Here I am praying and fasting, begging you to use me. You told me what You want me to do, and I blow it. Give me another chance. If You really want me to pray for her, have her come back in. I finished praying, walked halfway up to the front of the store, and she came walking through the front door, saying she forgot her coat. I knew why she had come back.

I told her that God wanted me to pray for her. A little surprised, she stopped, looked side to side, and said, "About what?" I said, "Do you believe Jesus died and shed His blood to forgive us for our sins? Do you believe if you ask Him to forgive you, He will?" She said, "Yes," and I said, "Okay, you shouldn't have any problem with me praying for you." She agreed. We went in the back, and I led her in a sinner's prayer. I was overjoyed and asked her how she felt. Some people say you shouldn't go by your feelings, but when you encounter Jesus for the first time, you're going to know. What she said next shocked me. She said, "I feel like myself. I don't feel like Kelly is anywhere around." I said, "Kelly.... who's Kelly?" She said, "Well, you know those people with two personalities?" I said, "a schizophrenic?" She replied, "Yeah, I'm schizophrenic."

It was then that God told me she had a spirit and to cast it out of her. She told me that when she was twelve years old, she and some friends were involved in a séance in a barn in Missouri, and ever since then, Kelly had been with her. She described Kelly as a little girl with long dark hair. She said she'd been in jail and attempted suicide because of her. As she was telling me all this, she stopped, smiled, and said, "This is really weird."

I thought, nothing can be more weird than what you're telling me. She paused and said, "Kelly wants to meet you." I thought, oh she does, huh? This is awesome! I knew Kelly couldn't hurt me, and I was fascinated with the thought of talking with this thing. Immediately, God told me not to have a conversation with it. It wanted to distract me from why He had exposed her to me that day. I said, "Well, I don't really care what Kelly wants, she's fixin' to leave." (fixin' to is a Texas phrase I picked up.) She told me Kelly wouldn't leave, that she'd told her to leave countless times over the past eight years, and she wouldn't. I said, "She doesn't have a choice. She's leaving, and she knows it. The only question is when." I asked her if she was ready. I had never been in this situation, but I knew God put me here. I put my hand on her forehead and said, "Kelly, God has exposed you this day. You've tormented this girl for the past eight years. In the name of Jesus, I command you to come out." That's all I knew to say. I asked her how she felt now. She said, "She's GONE!! When you were praying, I could feel her screaming inside of me." I won't lie, I felt like one of the Avengers! I know exactly how the disciples felt when they returned to Jesus, saying, "Lord, even the demons submit to us in your name." Luke 10:17 NIV. I started looking everywhere for these things!

Sometime later, I was talking to a friend of mine (I won't name him, but will refer to him as Greg). He had the worst stuttering problem I had ever heard. I said to him, "Maybe your stuttering isn't physical, maybe it's spiritual." He said, "Do you think?" I said, "I don't know, but we can find out. I'll just command anything not of God to reveal itself."

These things like to hide, but they have to reveal themselves when commanded to in the name of Jesus. Deliverance is serious business and shouldn't be taken lightly. I wouldn't recommend trying this as some type of parlor trick. A few days later, Carol and I went over to his house. He and his wife went to the same church we were attending. As soon as I prayed, "If there is any spirit not of God inside of Greg, in the name of Jesus, I command it to tell me its name." Immediately, he tensed up, and his eyes rolled back in his head.

One by one, they started telling me their names. It was bizarre to say the least. One after the other, as I addressed them, they left. This went on for hours. I was exhausted and wasn't prepared for this. I told the last one three times to tell me its name. It said Ose in a long, distorted tone. Three times it said the same name. Carol spoke up and said, "Vinal...., It's telling you its name is Ose." I laughed and said, "Well, that's a stupid name." This thing started growling at me, and would have ripped my head off if it could have. It was mocking God, mocking me, saying it was stronger than I was. I responded with maybe you are, but *"Greater is He who is in me than he who is in the world." 1 John 4:4 NASB* and in the name of Jesus, I command you to come out. It wouldn't leave. I wasn't spiritually prepared for this. It was a humbling experience.

I was exhausted and had a massive headache. Age and treachery will overtake youth and zeal. Frustrated, I asked God why it wouldn't leave. He reminded me that he had asked me to fast that day, and I didn't. When the disciples asked Jesus why they were unable to cast out one particular spirit.

He told them, *"However, this kind does not go out except by prayer and fasting" Matthew 17:21 NKJV.* As previously stated, some translations omit the word fasting.

I confessed to everyone that I had felt led to fast that day and didn't. Greg, his wife, and Carol had all felt led to fast that day and brushed it off. The next day, we all fasted, and Ose left without a fight.

Fourteen years later, I was on Wikipedia researching the names of demons. Guess whose name I saw? Ose. It said he was the president of hell and had between three and thirty legions of demons under him. My oldest son was looking over my shoulder, pointed and said, "Dad, look, there's Ose! That's why he wouldn't leave, you were messing with one of the big boys." I called an employee who wasn't a believer the night I found the Wikipedia page and told him to open the link I'd just sent him. It freaked him out. I had previously told him the story. He knew I didn't make up the spirit's name and had even said it was a stupid name. I've since learned not to go looking for a fight. The Apostle Paul allowed the woman with the fortune-telling spirit to follow him for days before telling it to leave. Book of Acts chapter 16:16-18. Stay away from fortune tellers, psychics, mediums, astrology, etc. They will take full advantage of any access you give them. Leviticus 19:31

They want you to seek their guidance and counsel and not the Most High God on behalf of your life. Don't be impressed just because they know certain names or things from your past. Why wouldn't they? They were around when things happened. These things are eons old and are allowed to be here for a time. I had an employee who was a Noahide (they follow the seven laws of Noah) ask me once why I don't send them to the abyss when I cast them out like Rabbi's do. I told him that Jesus didn't, and He's my example. Once, when the spirits asked Him if He was going to send them to the abyss before the 'appointed time,' He didn't, but rather cast them into a herd of swine. Luke 8:31-33

When the angel was sent to Daniel in the Old Testament (book of Daniel chapter 10), he told him he was delayed in bringing him his answer for twenty-one days by the Prince of the kingdom of Persia and had to call upon the Archangel Michael for help. He also mentioned having to battle the Prince of Greece after he left Daniel. How could an angel sent by God to deliver a message be delayed for twenty-one days by some principality? I don't know, but it's written. We know very little of what happens in the heavenly realm. Jesus also told Peter, **_"Satan has asked to sift all of you as wheat." Luke 22:31 NIV_**

But Jesus had interceded for them and told Peter that when he had repented after denying him three times, he was to go strengthen his brothers. Peter was oblivious to the request of Satan or that the conversation between Satan and God had even taken place. The Apostle Paul said, **_"We wrestle not against flesh and blood but against rulers, powers, authorities, and spiritual forces in the heavenly realms." Ephesians 6:12 NIV._** Even Paul was warned by The Holy Spirit not to go to certain places. Book of Acts 21:4.

I had another employee who thought he may have a spirit because of a vice he wrestled with, and asked me to pray for him. When I prayed, nothing happened. He said, "What does that mean?" I patted him on the shoulder and said, "It's all you, buddy. You can't blame everything on the devil." He said, "Well, now I feel bad."

We bought our second home in 1996. The couple we bought it from was going through a bitter divorce. Shortly after moving in, our children were seeing tall, dark images in the upstairs bathroom. I brushed it off and didn't think much of it. What we later learned is that the previous owner's teenage daughter had attempted suicide in that bathroom, I believe twice. One night, I was dreaming and saw faces morphing out of the ceiling. I remember they all had little heads and that one of them had a huge bulbous nose. As I was watching them, I thought, "You guys are pitiful," and actually kind of felt bad for them. (I knew they couldn't hurt me.) God told me they weren't after me, they were after our children. We had friends from church come over to pray and anoint our house and property with oil. The apparitions stopped immediately after that.

Our youngest daughter had something in her apartment when she was in college. One of her roommates said something pinned her in her bed, and she couldn't move. Carol and I drove down to College Station Tx, prayed over the house, blessed it, and anointed it with oil, and the disturbances stopped. Spirits don't go away by ignoring them. They need to be addressed.

When we were in Greece, a guy was sitting on the Metro in Athens, who I believe was demonized. I glanced over at him a few times, only to see him fixated on me. I turned to a friend I was with and said, "Did you see the man from Gadara over there?" (Luke 8:26-39) He said, "Yes, I did buddy…. Please do not engage him." I looked back at the guy who was still glaring at me and just smiled.

Questioning My Truth

I was discussing/debating Jesus being the Truth with a man once. I told him not to take my word for it but to seek the truth for himself with all of his heart. If you do, God will move mountains to reveal Himself to you. He said, "I've done that, and He didn't confirm Jesus as the truth. Are you calling me a liar?" I said, "Yes," ***"Let God be true but every man a liar."*** ***Romans 3:4 NKJV*** Myself included. I can explain it to you, but I can't make you understand it.

Shortly after getting saved, I ran into a friend I hadn't seen in probably six months. He was a guy from college I used to party with. He saw me in a coffee shop parking lot one night after we had closed our restaurant for the night. He ran up to me and said, "VINAL! What's going on man?" He asked me if I wanted to go to Boston. He was going to his brother's house to party all weekend and asked me if I wanted to go with them. I said, "I can't. I got saved, I'm a Christian now."

He took a few steps back, made a cross with his index fingers, and said, "Whoa, keep that stuff away from me, man. A friend of mine went crazy because of that." We went our separate ways. It was tempting to go with him, but I knew it would be too easy to fall back into that lifestyle. There is a proverb that says, ***"As a dog returns to its vomit, so a fool repeats his folly." Proverbs 26:11***

Fast forward nine years. Carol and I had moved to Texas and opened the restaurant. One Saturday night in January 1988, I was closing up with a high school girl. Her dad came to pick her up. We debated our differences in theology for a couple of hours. I knew enough of the Bible to hold my own, but he was older and a deacon at their church. I won't mention the denomination. He kept telling me I was deceived and didn't have the truth. The next day in church, that's all I could think about.

I kept praying, "God, I don't want to be deceived. The irony of deception is that those who are deceived don't know. How do I know I'm not? I have to know what I believe to be truth is really truth." A close friend of mine recently said to me, **"If you don't hunger for truth, a lie will satisfy."** We came home from church, and I was lying prostrate on my living room carpet, bawling my eyes out, crying out to God, telling Him I didn't want to be deceived, that I had to have the truth. Just then, the phone rang. Carol answered it and said it was for me. I said, "I don't want to talk to anybody. I could barely speak." She said, "You need to take this call." It was my old friend Steve. She knew him from when we all went to college together. I was surprised that he had found me. This was before the Internet. We were living in Texas, and he was living in California. After some small talk, Steve said, "I'll make a long story short." He had come home two days early from a business trip and caught his fiancée in bed with his best friend. His life plans and dreams came to a screeching halt. He said he was sitting on the edge of his bed with a gun in his hand, getting ready to blow his brains out. He said I can honestly say I prayed for the first time in my life. He said, "God, I don't even know if you're real, but if I'm going to die and meet you, I need to know what truth is." I can't explain it, but I heard a voice say, "Call Vinal." So, He just happens to call me as I'm praying this?

You can probably picture the smile on my face when people ask me, how do you know what you believe to be the truth is really the truth. Well, let me tell you a story....

Making Bricks Without Straw

arly August 1991. We had been in business for six years. The first few years were great financially and went according to plan. We had paid off our business loans, which were fourteen and a half percent, and even received the first 100 our city's Health Department had ever awarded. I don't know why, but the business had been in decline for about two years. I was always there, and the product and service were consistent. More than likely, it was the fact that there were now *thirty-five* restaurants within a mile of us as opposed to the dozen or so when we first opened.

The first Subway in the city opened on Main Street just around the corner from us in late 1986. Subway was doing more than double the volume we were. I started second guessing the decisions we had made. Thinking we should have stayed in Massachusetts for another year. We could have saved more money. We could have gone into the location where Subway was. That particular location was one of their highest volume stores. The plaza they were in wasn't even built when we opened. Every dime we had was invested in our location. Our 'boat', so to speak, was taking on water and slowly sinking. All of these thoughts had me on a downhill slope and picking up speed. The following is an analogy I relate to this type of thinking.

There was a picture where all but two inches in the center were covered up. Individuals were asked what they thought it was a picture of. Speculation and imagination varied greatly. One person thought it was a beautiful hillside with a stream winding through the middle. When the masking on the picture was removed, the actual picture was of the face of a cow. The exposed part was the tip of the cow's nose. We can fantasize about how our lives could have been had we made a couple of different choices or taken another path. The truth is, that will change nothing about where you are now. Stay focused on the day at hand and take each day as it comes.

When I had finished, I heard God ask in that still small voice. Are you done? Can I say something now? I thought, sure, go ahead. So what you're saying is you could have made better decisions without me. Didn't you pray about when to move and where to move to? Didn't I give you specific answers and even confirmations (cactus) as to what you were to do? Now you're second guessing those answers. If I order and direct your steps, that's all you can do. What about the people you met that came to know me the first year you were here, that you wouldn't have met had you waited a year? Or the ones you met in this location? The location I chose. Doesn't that mean anything to you? You're looking at things from a financial point of view, but I look at things from an eternal point of view. It was a humbling, but much needed rebuke.

Almost everyone second-guesses their life and the decisions they make. If we allow God to order our steps, we don't have the luxury or privilege of second guessing. We must not allow our past to be greater than our commitment to our future. Jesus told his followers not to look back. (Luke 9:62) We're also told to take every thought captive. (2 Corinthians 10:5) *"Trust in the LORD with all your heart, And don't lean on your own understanding. In all your ways acknowledge him, And he will direct your paths." Proverbs 3:5,6 HNV*

It was a Saturday morning, about 7 a.m., around the first week of August 1991. Carol was seven months pregnant with our oldest daughter. We had taken our two boys to a nearby hot air balloon festival. It was free, and I thought the boys would like it. We went by our store around 8 am to turn on the AC units. When I unlocked the door, I noticed standing water and mud in our dining room. Our store had flooded! It was also the only store in the plaza that had flooded. I told Carol to take the boys home. I had to stay and clean this up before we opened at 11 am. Because of our negative cash flow situation, not opening wasn't an option. I went to fill up the mop bucket, but there was no water. A water main in the alley between our plaza and another one had ruptured. The city crew had shut off the water in order to repair the break. They said it would probably take seven or eight more hours before they could turn the water back on. I used the water in the toilet and ice machine, but it was only enough for a few sq feet. Without the ability to rinse out my mop, I was simply pushing mud around.

Standing in the dining room, not knowing what to do, I prayed. "God, Israel made bricks without straw, (Exodus 5:18). I have to mop without water. How do I do that?" I looked outside and saw a small, foot-wide stream of water coming from the water main break going into the storm drain. I ran outside with my mop and rinsed it out in the clean water. I did this for around thirty minutes.

It was already close to ninety degrees outside. I was both exhausted and saturated. Some guy driving by saw me running through the parking lot with a mop. He turned around to find out what I was doing. He came in the front door and said, "What are you doing??" I explained, and he laughed. He said, "You're never going to finish!" I told him I had to do what I could and ran past him into the parking lot. When I came back in, he said, "I'll be right back." Around thirty minutes later, he returned driving a five-thousand-gallon Ram Jet city water truck, two mops, two buckets, and a helper. We filled up our buckets outside, and the three of us went to work. As they were picking everything up off the floor in the kitchen, they told me I'd worked hard enough and to go sit down, that they would finish. They were laughing as they went. One of them said, "If anyone had told me I'd be mopping the floor at Sub-Conscious, I would have told them they were crazy." As I was sitting on my bread table watching these two city employees mop my floor, God said to me, "That's how you mop without water." I was open by 11:00 a.m.

The Price of Unforgiveness

Around mid-August of 1991, we drove over to my sister's house on a Sunday afternoon. I really didn't want to go because financially, we were hanging on by a thread. We were renting a home from them and owed them three months back rent. The state had seized money we owed in back sales tax, and we were operating on a three to four-day negative cash flow. Which is why not opening the day the store flooded wasn't an option. When we arrived, I turned around in their driveway and went back home for fear that my brother-in-law would bring up what we owed them. Carol assured me that she had talked to him the week prior, and he said that if family can't help each other out in times of need, then what good is family? I knew full well what I owed him and hated the fact that I was unable to pay. I was working open to close six days a week, only because we were closed on Sundays. Carol talked me into going back over, so I reluctantly did. Carol was in the kitchen with Sandy and our two boys; he and I were on the back porch. He had been drinking. He asked me how business was. I said it was slow and that I was considering moving our location to one with better visibility and a higher traffic count, the only problem was that our rent would double. Keyword rent. He said, "Yeah… speaking of rent, when are you going to pay me?" My worst fear is staring me in the face. I said, "How do you propose that I do that?" He said, "Write a check." I told him it would bounce. Then go to the bank and take out a loan. Trying to diffuse where the situation was headed, I said, "Ok… that's what I'll do. I didn't know where you stood, and now I do."

He continued. "You know, you need to pay your bills, and if what you're doing isn't doing that, then maybe you need to find another job." I lost it. How dare he challenge what I had poured my life into? He hadn't worked for three years and was collecting a monthly stipend from a company he helped start. I stood up and laid into my brother-in-law. I was shaking and told him I wanted nothing to do with him ever again. I then told him I would give him back anything he had ever given me.

If he had stood up, I think I would have beaten him senseless. It was very ugly. Carol and Sandy heard us and started crying. The problem was, he was right. I owed him money and needed to be diligently seek God for my answer. Putting off paying him wasn't working. It just postponed the breakthrough God wanted me to have. Instead, I was using my brother-in-law as a backstop for my own frustrations.

You're going to question where you're at and if you heard God like you thought you had. Jesus said of John the Baptist, ***"Among those born of woman there is no one greater than John." Luke 7:28 NIV.*** Yet when John was arrested and imprisoned, he told his disciples to go ask Jesus if He was the one who was to come or if they should expect another. Jesus told them, ***"Go and tell John the things you have seen and heard: that the blind see, the lame walk, the lepers are cleansed, the deaf hear, the dead are raised, the poor have the gospel preached to them." Luke 7:22 NKJV.*** Jesus was referencing the messianic prophecy in Isaiah 35:5,6 and knew John would make the connection. Even John the Baptist questioned if he had heard God correctly. When Jesus was arrested, the disciples had no idea what was happening and abandoned Him.

In the Book of Zechariah it says, ***"Rejoice greatly, O daughter of Zion! Shout, O daughter of Jerusalem! Behold, your King is coming to you; He is just and having salvation, Lowly and riding on a donkey, A colt, the foal of a donkey." Zec 9:9 NKJV*** (This was fulfilled on Palm Sunday), Then in Zechariah 14, it says The Lord comes to do battle against the enemies of Israel. They are referred to as the two Messiah theories. Messiah Ben Joseph (peace) and Messiah Ben David (battle). The Israelites were expecting the Messiah Ben David.

They expected that when The Messiah came, He would establish His Kingdom. When a King comes riding a donkey, it signifies that he came in peace. If a King comes on a horse, he comes to do battle. The two Messiah scenarios in Zachariah were puzzling. Who could have envisioned a first and second coming? When Jesus returns, it will be as Messiah Ben David. According to Revelation 19, Jesus is returning on a horse.

A couple of days after the incident with my brother-in-law, Kathy Hayes, our pastor's wife came into our store. I told her what happened, and she started crying. She said, "You need to call your Covenant group leader, Ben Platter. Ben is a man of God, and you need a word from God." I held on to those words like a lifeline. I called Ben, and he agreed to meet with me the next morning at our store at 7 a.m. before he went to work. Ben was an executive with a large computer firm in Dallas. He came in, sat down, and told me all God was saying to him was that I needed to forgive my brother-in-law. I said, "But he's a jerk!!" Ben said, "I'm not saying he isn't, I'm just telling you what God is telling me." Reluctantly, after ten to fifteen minutes of defending my stance, I gave up and gave in.

Ben and I prayed. I told God I'd apologize and forgive my brother-in-law. Immediately, Ben had a word from the Lord and said, "My son, because you've agreed to do this, I will resurrect that which was dead." We finished praying, and I said, "What does that mean? What is God going to do?" Neither of us knew, but it was a sign of hope. I called my brother-in-law and told him I needed to talk to him. He agreed to come by the store the following Monday around 3 p.m. He asked my sister what I wanted to talk to him about. She told him she didn't know. I don't believe I had told her. When he came into the store, it was as if he had a wall surrounding him. He sat down, and I said, "I need to apologize for how I reacted and for what I said to you at your home." He didn't know what to say. I didn't have a backup plan or ace in my back pocket ready to pull out if he didn't accept my apology. It was unconditional. How do you fight humility? You can't. Especially when you're prepared for a fight. It caught him completely off guard.

Unforgiveness is huge. It's probably the most spiritually crippling thing most of us will face. It will drag you to the bottom and abandon you. It's lonely at the bottom. It's also dark, cold, there's a lot of pressure, and the fish down there are funny-looking. Jesus said, unless we forgive, we won't be forgiven. Ninety-nine percent of forgiveness is reaching the decision to do so. We may have reasons, they may even be justifiable, but we'll have no excuses.

A week or so later, on a Wednesday night at church, I went up for prayer. I still didn't know what God was going to do with my circumstances, only that He said He would "resurrect that which was dead."

George and Eunice Ferrell were the couple I went up to for prayer. Eunice asked if I had fasted. Initially offended by her question because I had been a Christian most of my life by this point. I told her yes, but probably not with the intensity I should have. On my way home, I told the Lord I would fast through Sunday concerning our business and what I should do next. In the Bible, we're told not to make rash vows. I was determined to stay focused and fast through Sunday. I had to do this with everything I knew to do. God gave me my answer and strategy about what to do regarding the business on Friday. On Saturday He asked me why I was still fasting. Because I said I would fast through Sunday. But you were fasting for direction, which I gave you yesterday. If you still want to fast, you can, but you don't need to. Within nine months, our business had more than doubled. We paid all our back taxes, rent, bills, and even bought our first home. God is faithful. Our breakthrough happened because I chose to forgive.

There's a story in Genesis 32:26 where Jacob wrestled with a man all night. At daybreak, the man said, "Let me go, for it is daybreak." Jacob said to him, "I'm not going to let you go until you bless me." The man asked his name. He said Jacob. He touched Jacob's hip, dislocating it. Then the man said, "Your name will no longer be Jacob but Israel because you have wrestled with God and men and have prevailed."

Too many times, we reach a point in life where our circumstances overwhelm us. We face a wall that's too high to climb, we can't seem to be able to get around it, and we can't break through. Things that once worked fail to have the impact and results they once had. Struggle seems to be a law of growth. We get discouraged, frustrated, start to get complacent, and eventually apathetic. What we need to do is to be like Jacob and hold on and tell God, "I'm not going to let go until you bless me." When we have done all that we know to do, we're told to stand firm. Maybe our new name is waiting on the other side of that wall. The Bible says God will make a way where there seems to be no way. In the Old Testament, there's a man named Gideon (Book of Judges chapter 6). Gideon was standing in a ditch threshing wheat when God called him a "Mighty man of valor." Gideon saw himself threshing wheat in a ditch, hiding from his enemy so they wouldn't come steal it. God saw Gideon for who he truly was.

When my brother-in-law was dying, I went into his room and sat down next to him. He wasn't conscious and was barely breathing. I prayed, "Lord, I don't want anything he ever did towards me to be held against him on my account. I forgive him." I can't emphasize enough the power of forgiveness. It's a choice we make. We don't have to, but it's critical in determining who we become. We may have reasons, but we'll have no excuses when we stand before God. Jesus said unless we forgive, we won't be forgiven. Jesus Himself is our ultimate example of this. While He was being crucified, His enemies were cursing, mocking, and still spitting on him. He said, "Father, forgive them, they know not what they do." Forgiveness and unforgiveness are both choices we make. We hurt others and are hurt by others, both intentionally and unintentionally. Hurt people, hurt people.

Craig Lemley, a pastor I know, said, **"If you never heal from what hurt you, you'll bleed on those that didn't cut you."**

Proverbs says to guard our hearts, this we seldom do

The treasure there's too often shared, with many not a few

Our motives may be selfish, and other times just blind

Once that door has been unlocked, the soul in ties it binds

Some say that time will heal all wounds, with this I disagree

God restores the deepest hurts, the price a bended knee

I myself am guilty of, the hearts of others marred

I pray the Lord restore them too, and heal the ones I've scarred
©

God sends an Intercessor

It was November of 1993, and our business was busier than ever. I had hired a manager to lighten my load. He had worked for a long time for a friend of mine, managing his Domino's Pizza franchise two doors down from me. We were back to struggling to make ends meet. I suspected my manager may have been stealing from me, but I didn't want to believe he would do that. He used to bring in Susan B Anthony dollars and half dollars, asking if he could cash them in. Surely no one cashing in change would be stealing. Carol was seven months pregnant with our fourth child. A woman named Linda, whom Carol had worked with in Massachusetts, called us out of the blue after eight years. She had since moved to Asheville, NC, and was attending a church there. She told Carol that a woman in her congregation named Marty had taken a bus to Dallas with her six-year old son because God told her to.

Marty didn't know why, only that she knew God told her to go to Dallas. Linda said that Marty was very prophetic. Marty was staying at the Motel 6 at 635 and I35 in Dallas. Linda asked if we'd call and check on her. I called and told her she could stay with us until God revealed to her why He wanted her in Dallas. When she got in the car, she handed me twelve dollars. She said, "God told me to give you this." I said I don't want any money. She insisted I take it. Reluctantly, I accepted it, figuring it was for gas. When we arrived at our house, the electric company was there to shut off our electricity. We had written the check, but had waited one day too long because of our cash flow situation. I said, "Wait, I have the check." He said ok but there was a reconnect fee on top of that. That fee was twelve dollars. Carol and I knew immediately that Marty was supposed to be staying with us. We didn't know why, only that she was.

Marty spent her time with us helping Carol with the children, laundry, and housework. She also prayed and fasted for us. She didn't eat anything for the first nine days she was there! Several times, I asked her to please eat something. She told me no, that the Lord hadn't released her yet. I had fasted countless times, but never on behalf of a breakthrough for someone else. It was a very humbling experience, to say the least. God sent a complete stranger to us from a thousand miles away, to fast, pray, and do battle in the spirit on our behalf. We were drained from the constant, seemingly never-ending struggle.

There's a story in Exodus 17:12-14 where Moses' arms grew tired, so Aaron and Hur held them up until sundown during a battle against the Amalekites. I am by no means comparing myself to Moses, by the way. Marty wrote the following note at the end of her fast. I still have it.

Carol and Vinal

"Thus saith the Lord

For I the Lord love justice; I hate robbery and wrong. I will faithfully reward my people, Vinal and Carol, for their suffering and make an everlasting covenant with them. Their descendants shall be known and honored among the nations. All shall realize that they are a people God has blessed."

Marty stayed with us for approximately 2 weeks. I took her back to the bus station, and despite trying to reconnect, we never saw or spoke to her again. Carol and I even tried locating Linda (Carol's former coworker), but weren't successful. I caught my manager red-handed stealing from me the following week. He denied it. I said, "I know you've been stealing. I forgive you.

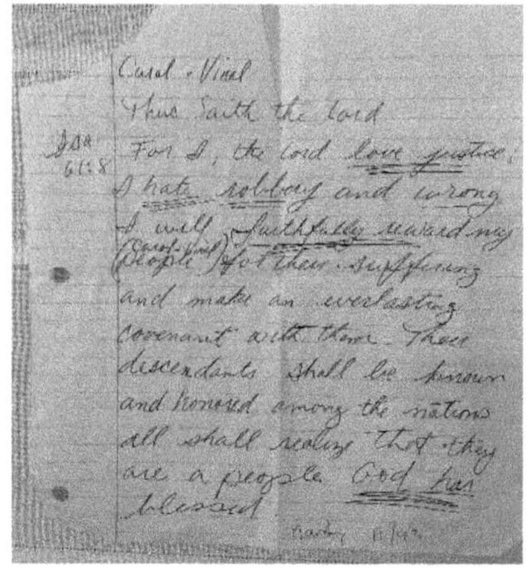

What you need to do is confess it and get on with your life." He handed me his key and walked out. Two years later, he mailed me a confession/apology letter and included a money order for the money he'd stolen.

Our Daily Bread

In mid January 1994, I called my baker on a Thursday afternoon and told them I needed a hundred and fifty, two-foot rolls for the weekend. His wife answered and told me they weren't baking bread that day because their help didn't show up. I said, "Excuse me? What am I supposed to do for bread this weekend?" She said it's never happened before and that they were going to lose money too. I hung up and said, "God.... what am I supposed to do?" As clear as day He said, "Learn to bake your own bread." I said, "TODAY?? Right now??" There was silence. I felt like one of those trains in WW2 getting strafed by a plane. I was completely vulnerable and felt sick to my stomach for the next two hours. My baker later called me and said we'd get our bread.

I knew what God had said, and I needed to look into baking my own bread. I called a man I used to go to church with in Massachusetts. I had visited him the previous summer while we were there. He had told me then that God told him to start baking. He shared a basic bread recipe with me that I had to tweak.

I would come home around ten o'clock each night and experiment with different bread formulas. When baking, all the conditions need to be consistent and precise. You only know how you did after it's baked. I later learned in a food handlers certification course that bread dough is also the only food where harmful bacteria don't multiply. Harmful bacteria need three factors in order to thrive: temperature, moisture, and a neutral PH level. Which is why food that is pickled or dried is safe when left at room temperature. Bread dough is room temperature, has a neutral PH, and has adequate water. Scientists don't know why dough is an exception. I've wondered if it's because Jesus refers to Himself as the Bread of Life?

After two weeks of experimenting, I was ready to give up. I just couldn't make it consistently turn out the way I needed it to. Then Dallas had an ice storm. I couldn't get any bread delivered the next day. Fortunately, I had enough bread to carry me over. I believe it was God showing me and confirming just how dependent and vulnerable I was. My mom was in town for the birth of our fourth child. Bless her heart, she would come for a month just before Carol was about to deliver. She would stay up with me night after night until 2 a.m., making bread. She used to ask Carol, "Do you think Vinal will want to bake bread when he gets home tonight?" Her answer was always, "Probably mum." On my twelfth attempt, I baked the perfect loaf!! I was excited. I can do this!! What I didn't know was that baking my own bread was going to reduce my overall food cost by six percent. That was the equivalent of two mortgage payments per month. Maybe that's why it's called dough.

I bought a double-door convection oven, a proofer, a Hobart floor mixer, a dough sheeter, a stand-up freezer, and baking pans. My baker came in to deliver bread one night, saw some of the equipment, and said, "You're going to start baking your own bread, aren't you?" He asked if what his wife said scared me. I said, "She scared me a little too much, Lou." I had all the baking equipment paid for in less than a year. I was now self-reliant.

The Loss of our Son

In 2005, Carol was pregnant with our eighth child. It was a boy. We had decided to name him Timothy. Carol told me early on in her pregnancy that she wanted to use an OB with this pregnancy. We had used a midwife for our three previous births and had them at home. I told her that was fine and that it was her decision. She went to her OB on November 24th. He said the baby was healthy and doing great. He told her she was at term but that if she didn't go into labor by Sunday, the 28th, he wanted to do a C-section, which we agreed to. He said, your body is very good at delivering babies, so I feel like we should let it happen naturally. Sunday morning, Carol said, something's not right. We need to call the midwife. Allison came over and checked his heartbeat. After five minutes or so, she said she couldn't find a heartbeat. I said, "Well, keep checking. We know it's there." I was talking to Timothy the whole time.

Hey buddy…today's the day!! We can't wait to meet you." Allison said, "Guys…I seriously can't find his heartbeat. We need to go to the hospital right now." What is this?? No!! He will live and not die!! God!! I need a word!! The Bible says, faith comes by hearing the word of God. Romans 10:17 The word used in Romans for word in the original Greek is rhēma. "That which is or has been uttered by the living voice, thing spoken, word." We can't create rhēma. Thinking you can, will get you into a lot of trouble. The prophets in the Bible only spoke what God told them to say. Even Jesus said, He only said what the Father told Him to say.

I called a couple we went to church with on our way to the hospital to ask them to pray, and left a message. I was crying uncontrollably and didn't even remember what I said. She played the message when she got home and contacted Carol a day or two later. Carol told her I felt awful for leaving a message like that. She said, "You tell him not to be, he has no idea how timely his message was." Thomas and I both had bad days and were feeling mistreated and victimized by life. When I played his message, my heart broke, and I just started crying. When Thomas got home, I played it for him. I said to him, "We don't have problems, we could be going through this right now."

Two people in the maternity ward on Sunday night asked me what we had. I told them our son didn't make it. That's the last thing someone in the maternity ward expects to hear. One young man just had a baby girl. I told him to take good care of that little girl. She's here for a reason. Life is a gift, not a given. The other person was a grandfather. He spent ten minutes talking about his twin granddaughters and showed me all the pictures. Then he asked, "What about you?" When I told him our son didn't make it, he burst into tears. He looked at me intensely and said, "I lost a son twenty years ago. Don't let it harden your heart." He quickly composed himself, turned away from me, and went back to his laptop. There were also three newborns on the news found locally that week that had been thrown away. One was found in a dumpster, and another one was found in a trash bag in a local lake by some guy who just happened to be walking by. A few weeks before Timothy was to be born, Carol asked me to write a birth announcement poem, which I thought was a great idea. I wrote it as a father's blessing on his son. This is the poem.

TIMOTHY JOSEPH PIERS

Our Baby Boy arrived today, as pure as pure can be

Untainted by the world out there, his eyes have yet to see

Let not his heart be troubled, as he puts trust in Thee

Reveal Your truths and plan for him, each time he bends his knee

Place in him a humble heart, compassion, hope, and love

May he be bold and full of faith, yet gentle as a dove

Guide him through each storm in life, as each one comes his way

May wisdom's voice reveal to him, his path from day to day

I don't know what his future holds, I do know it's ordained.......
©

I stopped writing the poem at this point, three weeks before he was born. Carol read it and thought it sounded a little morbid and wanted it to be something joyous and celebratory, so I stopped. It turned out to be prophetic. His future, unknown to me, was ordained. I finished the poem after he died with the following couplet.

I wrote this poem three weeks ago, not knowing this would come

This pain and grief someday will cease, farewell to you my son.

God did speak to me. Just not the words I wanted to hear. My prayer was, "God if you want a revival, raise an evangelist son from the dead. They won't be able to shut me up." He told me to go read the poem.

I didn't know Timothy didn't have a future here, but I did know his future was ordained. *"The righteous perish, and no one takes it to heart: the devout are taken away, and no one understands that the righteous are taken away to be spared from evil." Isaiah 57:1 NIV* I read Timothy's poem at the funeral, and there wasn't a dry eye in the place. One man came up to me afterwards and said, "When I walked in and saw your seven children standing at that tiny casket, that was all it took to break me."

A few weeks after Timothy died, I woke up at 3:34 a.m. The Lord told me to pray for Carol. I reached over and put my hand on her and started praying silently. God said, "Pray out loud." I prayed softly, telling God to let her know that Timothy didn't die because of anything she did or didn't do. That she wasn't to blame in any way. That there was nothing we would have done differently, etc. When I finished praying, she said, I was being tormented that it was all my fault. Everything you prayed nullified what was tormenting me. How could I have possibly known that?

Events happen in each of our lives that hit us like a freight train. Timothy's death was the hardest thing we've ever dealt with. I did take the next day off from work, but went in on Tuesday at 8 a.m. to make bread. Not one of my employees showed up. I had about fifteen orders (one order alone was for a dozen sandwiches), and three of the orders were deliveries I had taken before we even opened. It never occurred to me that my driver wouldn't show up. My dining room was full. I had to take the phones off the hook in order to make the orders I already had.

People were paying with credit cards. Each time they did, I had to put one phone back on the hook. As soon as I did, it would ring with another order. Nothing was stocked or prepped from the night before. In addition to taking and making every order, I was having to make tuna, fill dressing containers, cut tomatoes, bake bread, slice ham, cheese, and steak on the same slicer. I was a master at coordinating twenty things at once. But this was a nightmare, and I was on overload. I went outside twice and just started crying. God, I can't handle this. Meanwhile, Carol was alone in the hospital. I should have been there with her.

Most of our customers were long-time regulars. One after the other, they would ask if we had the baby yet. I would tear up as I told them what happened. One customer came in the back to cut tomatoes and filled dressing containers for me. A few days later, Carol made a sign explaining what had happened so I wouldn't have to talk about it. When they'd ask, I'd point to the sign. As they read it, they'd start crying.

I was in Massachusetts four months later, in March 2006, visiting my mom in the hospital. I felt prompted to visit another woman there. She was my sister-in-law's mother. I'd never met her before, but I felt like God wanted me to go see her. She had been given twenty-two units of blood for hemolytic anemia and was told there was nothing more they could do for her. I walked in and introduced myself. She said, "Oh, I heard about you losing your baby. I am so sorry. I lost a son forty-three years ago, how did you ever forgive God?" Wow, forty-three years and she'd never forgiven God!! King Solomon said a stillborn child is a mystery. King Solomon, the wisest man to ever live didn't even know the answer. We must guard our hearts. ***"Above all else, guard your heart, for everything you do flows from it." Proverbs 4:23 NIV***

I explained the Gospel to her and our need for forgiveness and to be forgiven. She said, "You make it sound so simple dear." I said it really is. We complicated it. She only opened up to me because she was all too familiar with that pain. God used Timothy's death to break through the wall she had built around her heart. We prayed together, and she forgave God and herself. She went on to live another eight years! I can't emphasize enough the power of forgiveness.

How God dealt with my Prejudice

In 1968, we moved to a new neighborhood. Being the new kid on the block is awkward. You just want to be accepted and fit in. I was raised in a Baptist home. I didn't know what I was until I asked another boy at church what we were. Our new neighborhood was predominantly Irish Catholic. This was during the 'Troubles' period in Ireland. A classmate at school told a story in front of the class about when his father went to Ireland. They asked him if he was Catholic or Protestant. He said Catholic. The area he was in was predominantly Protestant, so they beat him up. Later, he went to another part of the city where he was asked the same question. He thought he had learned what to say. He said he was Protestant. That section was Catholic, so he was beaten a second time.

One of the boys in our neighborhood was a bully. He asked me what I thought about the Pope's image being put on a coin. "Who's the Pope?" I asked. That was all it took to make me a target. There were around six or eight that started beating me up. My only memory of what happened is being on my back and them encircling me, kicking me in the head.

I spent about a month in Boston Children's Hospital with head injuries and had to wear a helmet while I was there because of it. I had no idea the impact it would have on me subconsciously. Whenever Ireland came up in my life, it would immediately stir something deep inside of me. Ironically, I married an Irish Catholic girl. God has a sense of humor.

In 2004, I was at a home church group meeting. A woman named Sheri Rhoades had invited me to the gathering. She is a missionary and a godly woman. A few months later, Sheri said she was going on a mission trip to Ireland and asked if I'd research the history of God moving in Ireland. Reluctantly, out of respect for her, I agreed. Driving home that night, I said, "GOD… WHY IRELAND?? I HATE IRELAND!! I couldn't care less if the place was nuked!!" He immediately asked me, "Do you know why?" It's because those kids who beat you up were Irish Catholics.

Immediately, I started crying. I repented and asked God to forgive me. I had no idea I had buried that. I tried to track down our neighborhood bully for more than thirteen years just to tell him I forgave him. I was finally able to locate him in August of 2017, almost fifty years after I was attacked. He was sitting in his garage when I pulled into his driveway. He walked out to see who I was, and I told him. He was thrilled to see me and gave me a hug. After twenty minutes or so of small talk, I brought it up. I said, "I need to forgive you for what you did." He had no recollection of it but apologized anyway. We talked for an hour or so and even picked some blueberries in his yard. He asked if he could call me so we could keep in touch.

A Jewel of Sudan

I flew to Boston in the spring of 2002 because my mom was in Beth Israel Hospital. We didn't think she was going to make it. When I walked into her room, her face was gray, and it scared me. I spent a week there on a cot in her room. An attendant came into her room one day to transport her to radiology. He asked in a beautiful accent, "Are you going to radiology?" Immediately, I asked him where he was from. He told me Sudan, and asked if I had ever heard of the Lost Boys?

I had just seen a special on the Lost Boys of Sudan, so I told him yes. He said, "I am a Lost Boy. My name is Khan Kai, but my Christian name is Gabriel." He saw a picture of my family on the wall and asked, "Is this your family? You have a beautiful family. What are their names?" I didn't want to talk about myself. I wanted to hear his story. Sudan is a war-torn country. Christians occupy South Sudan, and Muslims occupy the north. They've been fighting a civil war for decades. While he was taking us down to radiology, I did nothing but ask him questions. As he was telling me what he'd been through, I was in tears. I'm in tears again as I type this. His story had a powerful impact on me, I've tried several times over the years to locate him to follow up. I was able to reach someone at Catholic Charities in Boston that remembered him, but he couldn't give me his contact information due to privacy reasons. I wrote the following poem about the brief, divine appointment I had that day.

A JEWEL OF SUDAN

I met one time a refugee, a Lost Boy from Sudan

A handsome and a gentle soul, who said his name was Kahn

Standing tall at 6'3", his skin was like charcoal

His eyes and teeth were white as snow, I'm sure so was his soul

He'd not have said to me a word, unless I dared to ask

Reluctantly he shared with me, his wounded brutal past

I was aware of many things, the Sudanese had seen

Both He and I did wonder why, we failed to intervene

I asked Him where his family was, if they too did survive

He told me that he did not know, if they were still alive

He said that when the soldiers came, how they did maim and kill

As he described the horrors there, my eyes began to fill

He told me in his county that, two million souls have died

Because they chose to follow Christ, their own lives they denied

He said he wound up in Kenya, a mission took him in

Now orphaned in a foreign land, new life must now begin

He said he went through all of this, when he was only seven

Truly God has set aside for him, a special place in Heaven

What did impress me most of all, was that his heart's not hard

His love for God and faith in Christ, he could not disregard

I simply can't imagine how, nor can it be explained

How one could suffer through so much, his heart remain
unstained

Kahn Kai is just one precious soul, that God ordained I meet

Once I had heard what he'd been through, my trials can't compete

So next time that you're feeling down, remember my friend Kahn

America is truly blessed, unlike those in Sudan ©

A letter Never Sent

A pastor friend in North Carolina, whom I've known for thirty-five years, called me asking if I could help a man named Rick in his congregation with a product he had come up with. I told him I didn't know, but I'd do what I could. Rick and I hit it off from the start. He is the brother I never had. He hadn't spoken with his dad in years. Rick had written him a letter about the struggles and differences they'd had through the years. He didn't like what he had written and put it in his dresser drawer. He would take it out periodically to edit and even rewrite the whole letter. The letter stayed in his dresser, and he never sent it. His sister called him one night and told him, "Daddy passed away." He was crushed that he never sent his dad the letter. I wrote the following poem for him. He asked me to share it with anyone and everyone so they wouldn't make the same mistake he made.

A LETTER NEVER SENT

I wrote my dad a note one day, expressing all my thoughts

Reminding him of memories, through time he may forgot

Differences that we had had, tried to cloud my mind

I had to rise above that place, and leave the hurts behind

He is the only dad I have, the only that I'll know

I had to tell him how I felt, before his time to go

I didn't like what I wrote down, I set the note aside

I'll write another someday soon, emotions choked by pride

The note stayed in my dresser drawer, the letter never sent

The days turned into months then years, I don't know where time went

I got a phone call late last night, they told me he was gone

I sat there helpless wondering, why did I wait so long

Life's not supposed to end this way, I thought I'd have more time

I put it off one day too long, the blame is solely mine

Time is a precious gift we have, that needs be better spent

Don't let a chapter in yours be, a letter never sent ©

I try to share the poem on social media every Father's Day. I remember one comment from a woman I went to high school with, who wrote something along the lines of, OMG…. Vinal, your poem brought me to tears! I'm calling my father tomorrow. What more could I ask for?

I recently talked with someone who had a lot of resentment towards his father. A lot of it was justified. I said, "So what are you going to do with that?" That happened more than forty years ago. Holding onto it will cripple who you are and affect who you become. You will unintentionally and unknowingly pass those traits onto your own children. Is that what you want? The Bible says, *"Honor your father and your mother, that your days may be long upon the land which the Lord your God is giving you." Exodus 20:12 NKJV.* It's not a suggestion. It's an unconditional commandment. It's also the first commandment with a promise. Our responsibility and command is to honor our parents regardless of whether or not it's due to them. The Apostle Paul instantly apologized for rebuking a high priest once. *"I did not know, brothers, that he was the high priest, for it is written, 'You shall not speak evil of a ruler of your people.'" Acts 23:5 ESV*

Ask God how you can do that. He will show you. You do what you can, and let God do what only He can do.

I spoke with one man in his mid-forties, whose dad was terminally ill. I told him he needed to talk with his dad before he passed. He agreed, but said he's never been one to talk much, which was true. He was a man of few words. I believe God gave me the words to explain it to him. I told him that when that door closes, you can never open it again. Set the time aside while you still can. If you don't know what to say, ask him this question. "I don't know what it's like to be without a father, you do. Is there anything you wish you had talked with your dad about before he died?" He waited three weeks to have their conversation. They talked for hours. He told me his dad told him things he never knew, and even that he was proud of him for the first time in his life. His father passed away three days after they spoke. He is forever thankful he set the time aside to meet with his dad.

In the course of writing this book, I was talking to someone I've known for a long time about this chapter. I had no idea of the resentment he had towards his father. He told me when we hung up, he started thinking about his dad and just started crying uncontrollably. He told me he hated his father. We didn't discuss the reasons why, only that he had to forgive him. He said after he let go of his unforgiveness, he felt like a huge weight had been taken off of his shoulders. We later laughed when he referred to it as his Chris Farley "How could I have been so stupid?" moment.

A couple of years ago, I was invited to a wedding in another state. I initially told them I wasn't going to be able to attend. The groom wanted to invite his grandfather, whom he hadn't seen for several years. His father and grandfather hadn't spoken to each other for probably six years. I called the grandfather and asked if he wanted to go. He said he would like to, but didn't want his estranged relationship with his son to be a distraction during the wedding. I said I would attend the wedding with him and be a buffer between the two of them. Both he and his son thought that was a good idea. The two of us flew in and landed about fifteen minutes apart. We rented a car and checked into our hotel. The three of us agreed to meet up at a local restaurant. When his son came in, his father stood up, and they just hugged each other and wept for several minutes. I took a picture and sent it to them with the caption, "No words needed."

During our premarital counseling, the pastor asked Carol and I how our relationships were with our parents. I said, "My mom is great, and my dad's a jerk." I had determined in my early teens that I could never make him happy, so I had quit trying and simply tuned him out of my life. The pastor said I needed to work on my relationship with him because he wouldn't always be there. Little did I know he'd be gone in less than three years. Our relationship was restored the last year of his life as he battled cancer. ***"And he will turn the hearts of the Fathers to the children, and the hearts of the children to their fathers," Malachi 4:6 NKJV***

This is the poem I wrote for my dad.

THE PATRIARCH

Today my life changed drastically, our Patriarch has died

It's up to me to carry on, my family's faith and pride

I was then just twenty four, no children of my own

I wish that they he could have met, before God called him home

The radio and children play, right now the news is on

It's like the world is unaware, our Patriarch is gone

The Dr came into your room, and shared with us the news

Then left us all in deep despair, our hope dazed and confused

How does someone prepare himself, to live through this ordeal

I've never had to walk this path, what should I think or feel

All my life you have been there, how quickly things have changed

I'm emotionally exhausted, my priorities rearranged

I'm thankful for the times we had, and talks of days gone bye

To share our love and just hold hands, and gaze into his eyes

Sometimes at night when others sleep, I'll lie awake in bed

And reminisce of times we had, and little things you said

The people that I meet today, may not know how I grieve

Unless they too have walked death through, their hearts could
not conceive

At times I want to be alone, at other times cry or shout

Or just reflect on things you said, it's you I'm now without

The last few months he lived his life, he told men of God's grace

Forgiveness he could never earn, through Christ simply erased

Some said they couldn't look at him, he saw into their soul

He told them how God sent His Son, in case they'd not been told

He knew that he had little time, all saw this in his eyes

He simply shared with all his heart, emotions undisguised

I've wondered if God lets him see, what my life's since become

One question I've asked more than once, why my dad died so young

I'm told by those who've gone through this, that time will heal my wound

I hope and pray this to be so, right now it's just too soon

To lose someone so close to you, the pain down deep inside

Until you know of this firsthand, in words I can't describe

Till death has touched your life my friend, you'll not have much to say

These words I write I know first hand, for me that day's today

I'm thankful for those precious times, when we both shared our hearts

I pray all children do the same, before their dad departs ©

I personally know two men who are great fathers from South Central LA who grew up fatherless. The odds of them getting out of there and making something out of their lives were practically zero. God made a way for them where there seemed to be no way. It wasn't easy, but they stayed focused and determined. God is a father to the fatherless

We are the Clay God is the Potter

Like it or not, we are clay in the hands of the potter. I don't know about you, but I like to have input as to what God is making with me. If I like what I think He's doing or where He's taking me, I'm fine. Having been self-employed my whole life, I've had my share of surprises.

I was visiting my sister-in-law's church in the northeast several years ago. The guest speaker was a potter. As he was turning a large block of clay on his potter's wheel, he would relate it to our lives. He was constantly putting water on it to keep it moist and pliable. He would reach deep inside to hollow it out. He used different tools to dig out clay and discard what he didn't need as he went. His arm, at times, was deep inside, all the way to his shoulder. The analogy was that sometimes God needs to remove things deep in our lives, and the process can be uncomfortable. He was finishing what appeared to be a three-foot-tall, beautifully shaped vase any artisan would be proud of. All he had left to do was fire it in a kiln. The final step in the process.

He then took out a type of knife and removed eighty percent of the height. He folded up what he had cut off and discarded it in the pile of excess clay. He spent the last few minutes shaping his piece into a bowl. He asked the congregation, how many thought he was making a vase? Practically everyone raised their hand. He said, "I knew when I started I was making a bowl." We may think we know where God is taking us and even how He's going to get us there. The reality of it is, we are clay in the hands of the potter. I wanted to walk out right then. I didn't like his message at all. I like to know where God is taking me, how I'm getting there, the route He's taking me, and who's coming with me. It's taken me several years to learn that God truly wants what's best for me, and I have to trust Him. *"For we are His workmanship, created in Christ Jesus for good works, which God prepared in advance that we should walk in them."* *Ephesians 2:10 NIV*

The Church Moved By The Hand Of God

Around 25 years ago, I read the story of Swan Quarter Methodist Church in NC, and I've always wanted to visit the site. It's known as "The Church Moved by the Hand of God." In 2022, my sister moved to Florida, and I helped her drive her car there.

I told her the story of the church, and we decided to stop. It was roughly a two hundred and fifty mile detour. The current population of Swan Quarter is less than three hundred people. We probably only saw two or three cars on the road the whole time we were there. We parked in the back parking lot of the church and walked around the building. I was asking God about the people who built it and why He intervened for them the way He did. God is more concerned about people than He is about a building. God even let His own Temple in Jerusalem be destroyed not once but twice. The church was locked and pretty run-down. After thirty minutes or so, we went back to the car. As we were sitting in the car, a woman pulled in and parked probably a hundred feet away from us. I said, "God, I'd like to go inside. Have her ask us if we'd like to."

She got a package out of her truck and carried it into a separate building that shared the parking lot with the church. I thought that was to us not getting into the church. My sister said she had to use the restroom, so we decided to leave. We pulled onto the side street and drove to the intersection. I had forgotten to take a picture of the front of the church, so I pulled over and got out.

As I was getting back in the car, the woman drove out from the back of the church, turned onto the side street, and drove up alongside us. She pulled up, put the passenger window down,

and asked, "Did y'all want to go inside?" I said, "That would be awesome!" Oh, and is there a restroom my sister can use? She said of course, let me see if I can find the key. I don't remember seeing a place to stop for eighty miles or so on the drive there, and Swan Quarter was practically deserted. Suzanne found a key and gave us a personal tour, and showed us where the restroom was. I told Suzanne she was an answer to prayer, to which she replied, "Well, I don't know about that." I said, "No, you really are," and I told her what I had prayed. The church built a larger brick structure in 1913 connecting the two buildings. Both buildings are used for storage today.

This is their story.

In 1876 The Methodists in Swan Quarter NC, wanted to build a church for their growing congregation. Because Swan Quarter was a coastal town, in a low-lying area that was prone to flooding, they wanted it built on the highest ground possible. They found a piece of land where it would be high and dry.

When they approached Sam Sadler, the land owner. He refused to sell it to them. They settled on a lower parcel behind the old courthouse that was gifted to them by James Hayes. They built the church and had their dedication service in mid-September 1876. A hurricane hit the next day and ravaged the town. When the storm and wind subsided, the residents looked outside only to see the small Methodist church intact, floating down Oyster Creek Rd. The townspeople frantically attached ropes to it to keep it from floating away. It continued down the street, then made an inexplicable sharp right turn on Main St and traveled another two blocks. It came to rest in the center of the vacant lot they initially tried to buy from Mr Sadler, where it has remained to this day.

Just Talking to God

I was tiling my downstairs bathroom and was meditating on what I believed God had told me concerning things that would take place in my life that had yet to manifest. I was questioning if He had really said what I thought He had. Some of what He told me was years prior that simply hadn't happened. It was at this point that He said to me, Moses knew he was the one who would deliver Israel when he broke up the fight between the two Hebrews. Moses even killed an Egyptian who was beating a Hebrew slave. He then fled to Midian and raised sheep for forty years, yet Israel walked out of Egypt four hundred and thirty years to the day God said they would. When the time was right, God lit the burning bush and told Moses to return to Egypt.. I thought, Wow, Moses knew that forty years ahead of time? I'm sure Moses questioned if he had truly heard God about him being their deliverer during the years he was raising sheep. I set the tiles down, went into the kitchen and opened my Bible to Exodus to re-read the account. It doesn't say anything about Moses knowing that ahead of time. I was puzzled. Then I started to get scared, thinking I was making things up. I said, "God, how did I get here?" "I'm making things up now." The Bible says to not go beyond what is written. 1 Corinthians 4:6. I was really scared. About a minute later, I heard that still small voice. "You read Acts chapter seven a few weeks ago, go read it." It states, *"Moses thought that his own people would realize that God was using him to rescue them, but they did not." Acts 7;25 NIV*

Stephen.... First martyr of the church, the man who said he saw Jesus standing at the right hand of God, right before he was stoned to death. Acts 7:56 (Jesus had previously only said He was going to be seated at the right hand of God.) I don't know where you heard Moses knew that, but I believe you. That moment of despair lifted off of me. Stephen was a nobody in the church. He was a servant, yet was the first martyr. **"If you're waiting on God, do what waiters do: serve," Ann Voskamp.** The first shall be last and the last shall be first. This is a poem I wrote about Stephen.

STEPHEN THE SERVANT

Our hearts should be like Stephens, of whom the Apostles did ask

Who thought that to serve not beneath him, to him just his godly task

The church did appoint unto him, the widows and orphans to feed

To daily distribute them bread, and to any perhaps in need

His life was full of God's miracles, his anointing had people in awe

Chosen for his faith and love for the Lord, and God's hand on his life that they saw

Today some may think this is strange, or perhaps even think a demotion

To just pass out bread and to care for the church, to Stephen it was his devotion

You see Stephen was no small man, of great power and faith was he filled

He sought not to start his own ministry, only that which the Father had willed

I'm sure there were those in his life, that said, don't they know who you are?

A ministry of helps, a servant of others, just tell them that you are a star

Please tell them that this is beneath you, God's call on your life too intense

And then if they still won't believe you, we'll all then run to your defense

Stephen had long since died to self, his own will far removed

Selfless ambition with total submission, for the church his own martyrdom proved

In the end he was first to be martyred, for Christ His young church to die

To be last and not first, the least and not most, truly it was his heart's cry

Now Jesus with the Father in glory, yes seated at God's own right hand

Just read for yourself at his stoning, that Jesus himself did stand
©

Be specific when you pray

In 2006, our oldest daughter was a junior in high school and had qualified to compete in the state track competition. The competition was being held two hundred miles away in Austin. I told Carol that I didn't want her to take the Suburban in case there were any mechanical issues. I suggested we rent a car and she agreed. She said if we're going to rent a car, that she'd like to get one she'd enjoy driving. She was in the height of shuttling our seven children around to school, practices, their jobs, and church in our practical family vehicle. I asked her what kind of car she wanted.

She thought about it and said, "A Mustang would be nice." So, we prayed for a Mustang. We reserved one online a couple of weeks in advance for 10 a.m., to be picked up at the Avis location a few miles from our house. When the day came for them to leave, I called Avis around 9 a.m. to confirm we wanted a Mustang. The woman told me they didn't have any Mustangs and that the agreement stated "or similar vehicle." I told Carol what they said. She was naturally disappointed and said, "Where is God? I just wanted to drive something fun and special." I said, "It's only a car." As I was loading their luggage into our car, I said a simple prayer, "Lord, can you just get her a Mustang, let her know you care about the little details." We walked into the office and gave them our names. The woman said, "Oh Mr. Piers, I just tried calling you. They're on their way over from the airport with a Mustang." I looked at Carol, and she was beaming. A few minutes later, they pulled up with the Mustang. The woman said, "Wow, a convertible. I didn't request a convertible. You got lucky." Carol was smiling from ear to ear and said, "God did that for me." Several times then, when we don't think God sees what we're facing or going through, we say to each other, "Remember the Mustang."

A friend of my oldest son is a single dad. I had told him the story of the Mustang years ago and how we should be specific when we pray. Just recently, he texted me a picture, then called to explain it. He said his ex-wife had the children that weekend, so he was alone. He was feeling a little down and under the weather and didn't want to go out to get food.

He thought about my story of the Mustang, prayed, and told God he would like for someone to just bring him something to eat. A friend of his called him about twenty minutes later and asked if he'd eaten. If not, did he want to go grab a bite somewhere? He said he was feeling a little under the weather and really didn't want to go anywhere. His friend responded with, "I'm just going to bring you some food." He came over with baked chicken, roasted potatoes, asparagus, and bread. The picture he texted me was of the meal his friend had brought over. He was so excited that God answered his simple prayer request.

God wants us to be specific when we pray. Jesus repeatedly asked people, "What do you want me to do for you?" In our times of uncertainty, we reflect on those moments when God answered our personal specific prayers. I once wrote down all the positive and negative things in my life. It was during a time of despair when the negatives outnumbered the positives three or four to one. I found the list about a year later. ALL of the negatives were gone, but all of the positives were still there. No matter what you may be going through, it will pass.

In the course of writing this book, I've spoken to several friends. Many have said that they needed to write down the times they prayed, and God answered. Some have, and as they were recalling their own accounts, they were both encouraged and blessed.

God instructed Israel to write things down. The Bible is a book of stories. God had Israel place the Ten Commandments, Aaron's staff that budded, and some of the Manna he fed them with to be placed in the Ark of the Covenant as both a testimony and evidence to what He had done. At the Last Supper, Jesus said, "Do this in Remembrance of Me." We need reminders.

Carol and I recently reconnected with a precious couple we went to church with decades ago. I told them I was finishing up a book. The wife told us God told her she has five books in her. I said you need to write them. She said she told another 'friend,' and she laughed at her and said no one will want to read your book. She said that comment caused her to close up and shut down. This woman is a prayer WARRIOR and powerful intercessor!! She has incredible stories of seeing God move when she prays. I make it a point to ask how the book is coming when we talk.

I had an employee once try to trivialize one of my testimonies. I said, I understand you belittling that story, but it didn't happen to you. My question to you is, how many examples do you have where God confirmed your faith to you? He thought about it and said he didn't have any. A person with a testimony is never at the mercy of a person with a theory. Don't allow critics to affect you. Some people just like to argue. It is written, ***"Warn a divisive***

I highly recommend you to watch 'The Throne Room' by Graham Cooke on YouTube. It will forever change how you view the critics you have in your life. These testaments are memorials for when our faith and beliefs are questioned by us and are a testimony to others. Like the clay in a previous chapter, we'd like to know all the details about where God is taking us and why. We don't like being clay. Our job is to remain pliable so God can mold us into what He created us to be and wants us to become. A friend of mine once asked God where He was taking him. God answered him with, "If I told you, you wouldn't go." Would Israel have left Egypt if they knew they were going to spend the next forty years wandering in the desert? Would I have gone back over to my brother-in-law's house if I knew he was going to ask me for the money I owed him?

We like to go the shortest, quickest, most efficient route, even if we have to pay tolls along the way. God seems to prefer we take the scenic route so He can deal with things we've buried along the way like unforgiveness. Our beliefs and faith will be tested. God wants us to be sincere. Each one of us will stand before the Most High God and be accountable. Any self-righteous imperfections that may have fooled others will be exposed. We are all guilty of sin. Jesus alone is righteous, and His forgiveness is free. Ask Him for it.

Don't ask God a question unless you really want to know the answer. A man I know worked in a corporate setting. A coworker of his told him he had a lust problem. He denied it and laughed at the guy. Shortly afterwards, he was walking down the hall and was thinking about what his friend had said. He said to God, "I don't have a problem with lust.... Do I?" He had no sooner thought that when he walked into a glass door, spilling his coffee all over his shirt. He didn't see the door because he had turned to check out a woman who had just walked by. Immediately God said to him, "What do you think?"

In April 2006, a couple asked us to watch their dog while they went on vacation. As I was driving through the airport, I asked God if I should ask them for the one dollar exit toll. He clearly said, "No." They were talking about their trip and discussing things they may have forgotten. All I could think about was the dollar toll I didn't have. I told God again I didn't have a dollar on me, and I'd need it when I left the airport. He said, "Don't worry about it." I dropped them off at their gate and pulled up a few gates. I looked for loose change under my front mat and seat and found a dollar and seven cents in change. I had my dollar. When I got home, the couple had left a thank-you card on our island. Inside was four hundred dollars in cash.

A day or so later, a former restaurant customer contacted me. His marriage was on the rocks, and he was desperately trying to save it. He called me one morning and asked if I could drive into Dallas with him to deliver inventory to one of his customers. He asked me to bring my Bible. When I got in his truck, he said open up to Proverbs 3:27,28. It says, ***"Do not withhold good from those to whom it is due, when it is in your power to act. Do not say to your neighbor, "Come back tomorrow and I'll give it to you—when you already have it with you." Proverbs 3:27,28 NIV.***

He said, "I read that last night," and handed me a signed blank check. He said, "Fill it out for whatever amount you need for the month." I handed it back to him and said I wasn't going to do that. He said, "Then I will. How much is your mortgage?" What he didn't know was that we had just run out of money from the sale of the restaurant, and didn't know how we were going to pay our mortgage that month. I worked with him for over a year. He was paying me more than I earned at our restaurant. He was more than generous. He then lost his largest account, which was close to six figures monthly. It was then he told me he was a hundred and ninety thousand in credit card debt and didn't know what he was going to do. I said, "What are you doing? You can't afford to be paying me." I basically fired myself. He asked what I was going to do for income, and I told him God would provide, that he wasn't my source. I told him to bring me all of his debts. He set them on his island, and I prayed over them. I told God he had been exceedingly generous to me and I wanted his debts paid. Nothing happened immediately. When his house was on the verge of foreclosure, an uncle of his passed away and left him just under a million dollars. I don't know the exact amount, but it was enough to pay off the three hundred thousand he owed on his house, the hundred and ninety thousand in credit cards, put an additional garage on his house, buy a new truck, and still have two hundred thousand left over to spend on a hobby of his. When I found this out, I reminded God that I could use a little myself.

I had three signed contracts where I would earn anywhere from three hundred thousand to a million dollars in commission if they closed. I didn't dream these up, but found myself right in the middle of them. I met some very interesting and influential people. One meeting we had was with a Native American tribe. We wanted them to partner with us on government contracts. Our CEO and CFO asked me to remain outside to be praying everything went smoothly in the meeting. I had been in several prior meetings and knew what would be discussed. There was a huge grapevine near where we parked. I said, "Have I ever shared with you the spiritual lessons you can learn from a grapevine?" The CEO said, "We know Vinal, you've told us." I did a prayer walk around the property, then sat at a picnic table to read my Bible. A man pulled into the parking lot and parked around seventy-five feet away from me. As he was getting out of his car, I said, "Lord, if you want me to talk to him, have him come over here." He opened his trunk, took out his briefcase, and saw me. He walked over to me and said, "Do you have business with the nation?" I said yes, and told him three of my associates were inside, and told him what the meeting was about. We talked for around twenty minutes.

He said, "That sounds really interesting. I'm looking forward to hearing all about it." When I suggested he join the meeting. He said, "That's fine, I'll hear all about it." He told me how much he had enjoyed our conversation and asked what my name was. I asked him his name, and he told me and said he was the CEO of the Nation. I laughed and said, "I'm talking to the man himself." We both had a good laugh. I couldn't wait for the others to come out of their meeting. The three of them walked out of the building after being in there for over two hours. I was standing by the car and the grapevine just smiling.

I said, "How did your meeting go?" They said it went well, but we knew it was time to go when they started introducing us to everyone in the office. I said, "I had a good meeting too."

Our CEO chuckled and said, "With who, your grapevine?" I said, "No, actually, with Dennis Pxxxxxx, the CEO of the Nation." Our CEO said, "What?? How did you? Where did you? What did you say?" I laughed and said, "I was just out here praying, being among the least of us."

When our oldest daughter was graduating from high school, she wanted to go on a senior trip to Cancun with her girlfriends. Carol was sick to her stomach at the thought of something happening to her when she was there. Young girls are targeted by those looking to take advantage of them while they're there. I told Carol that she's 18 and earned the money to go by herself. We can't stop her. What we can do is pray that God let her experience that lifestyle in its full glory. Forbidding her to go could cause her to resent us for it and drive a wedge between us and Carol agreed. When we picked her up at the airport, her countenance was different. We got in the car, and I asked how her trip was. She said, "I wasted nine hundred dollars, I was everyone's mother!" Everyone was getting drunk and throwing up. One of them even threw up on her when she was helping them. She was watching her friends' drinks to make sure no one spiked any of them. She took people who couldn't walk back to the hotel. She said it was awful and reiterated that "She wasted nine hundred dollars." I said, "No, you paid for a life lesson." I believe that experience taught her things she stayed away from before she went off to college.

On a flight home from Texas Tech once, she sat next to a big kid who had just toured the college. She asked him if he went to Tech. Flattered, he said, "I'm only a junior in high school, you thought I was in college?" She said she didn't know. He followed up with, "I heard Tech is a big party school." She said, "Every school has a party crowd, if that's what you're looking for, it's there. If you want to focus on a great education, that's there too. You're the one who will choose which path you take." I said, "Honey, you potentially changed his entire direction in life."

One night, I was driving to Sonic Drive Inn to pick up one of our daughters from work. On the drive there, I wondered why nothing seemed to be coming to fruition, business-wise. I prayed for something to break regarding our finances. I told God, if provision was coming, have her bring me out a drink. That way, I'll know to keep hope. The Bible says, ***"Hope deferred makes the heart sick, but a desire fulfilled is a tree of life." Proverbs 13:12 RSV***

My daughter walked out of the store without a drink. I thought, well... I got my answer. She got in the car and said, "Did you want a drink?" I didn't know what to say. Confused, I said, "I don't know." She said, "Well, do you or don't you?" I told her I did and that I wanted a Cherry Slush. She went back in, came out, and handed it to me. I said, ok. I'm totally confused now, and I told her what I had prayed. She said, "I was going to make you a drink, but I didn't know what kind you wanted. Maybe God wants you to be more specific when you ask Him for something."

It was during this time that I went on a fast. As I previously stated, it says in the Bible not to make rash vows. I told God I wasn't going to eat until I got paid. Several days later, one of my business associates came up to me and handed me a thousand dollars in cash. He said I know you've been working hard and haven't seen any results, but he wanted me to have it as a token of appreciation. I said, "Are you saying I'm getting paid?" He said, "Yes, I know it's not much, just a little something." I then told him I had told God I wasn't going to eat until I got paid. He said, "Wow, that's pretty radical." I said, "I'm at a pretty radical place in my life."

A couple of years ago, we visited a new church. Carol and I felt like we should be plugged into a local church in our area. The pastor wanted to take me to lunch. We went to a local Tex Mex restaurant and sat outside on their patio. He was asking me how things were going and where I was at with the Lord. I told him there was a song titled "My Eyes are Dry" by Keith Green that summed up where I was at. These are the lyrics.

My eyes are dry..My faith is old.. My heart is hard

My prayers are cold.. And I know how I ought to be

Alive to You and dead to me.. Oh what can be done

For an old heart like mine.. Soften it up

With oil and wine.. The oil is You, Your Spirit of love

Please wash me anew.. With the wine of Your Blood

The chorus repeats.

That's the entire song. It's from 1978. Keith Green was killed in a plane crash in 1982. It was probably written during a dry season in Keith's life, when he had more questions than answers. I refer to those times as "Raising of Sheep in Midian," where Moses was until God lit the bush on fire and told him to return to Egypt. Israel walked out of Egypt four hundred and thirty years to the day God said they would. It's not a very popular message in some churches. If you don't tell the masses what they want to hear, they'll go down the street to pastor wonderful's church.

The pastor wasn't familiar with Keith Green or the song. About a minute or two later, he was talking about something, and that very song came on the speakers on the patio. I interrupted him and said, "Listen… listen!!" This is the song I just told you about!!" I was shocked. I think it kind of freaked him out. I don't ever remember hearing anything but Mariachi music when I'd been at that restaurant in the past. Certainly not a forty-five-year old song from a contemporary Christian artist that's been gone for over forty years. I believe it was God letting me know He knew exactly where I was.

Last year, I helped one of my sisters move from Massachusetts to Indiana so she could move in with her son and his family. The morning after we arrived, my nephew could only find one friend to help us unload the two U-Haul's. After we finished unloading the trucks, we were just sitting in the kitchen, taking a much-needed break. The guy who came over to help said this past year had been the worst year of his life. I was surprised because he barely said a word the entire time we were working. I asked him why, and he proceeded to tell me. His wife had filed for divorce and had a restraining order taken out against him. The court ordered him to have no unsupervised meetings with his two young children because his wife had accused him of being abusive and suicidal. He also had to sell their home because his wife wanted the money. She got fifteen thousand dollars, and he received around fifteen hundred, which went to his child support.

In addition, he had to get rid of the few guns he owned. The only one he had any attachment to was an old rifle his grandfather had given him. He said he'd never had a suicidal thought in his life until the last couple of months. My heart went out to the guy. I asked him if I could pray for him because I wanted God to intervene and move on his behalf. He said, "I don't really believe in God." I said, "Oh, I don't care, this is on me."

As soon as I started praying for him to see God move in his life, I broke down. God hates injustice! I could barely speak as I prayed. I felt like God let me experience a small portion of His compassion for him and his situation. It caught me totally by surprise and completely off guard. There are several examples of Jesus being 'moved with compassion 'in the New Testament.

Compassion in the original Greek is **Splanchnízomai.** This is the meaning according to the Strong's Lexicon.

Splangkh-nid'-zom-ahee; middle voice from G4698; to have the bowels yearn, i.e., (figuratively) feel sympathy, to pity:—have (be moved with) compassion. I have no idea what he thought about his friend's crazy uncle. When I finished praying, I told him I didn't know what God was going to do for him, but I knew he was going to see it first hand and he would know God intervened. He said he had a child custody hearing coming up on Monday. I called my nephew on Tuesday, and the restraining order regarding his children was dismissed by the court.

Praying for Rain and Thunder

On May 30, 2010, none of the deals I had been involved with were going anywhere. The economy was still recovering from the 2008 financial crisis. Money was tight, and groups were hesitant to invest their own capital. On Sunday morning, May 30, 2010, at 7 a.m. I went downstairs to make coffee before going to church. As it was brewing, I told God I needed a confirmation that provision would come this year. I said, "If it is, I want it to rain today, I want to hear thunder, and I want to get wet." I had no idea what the forecast was. I later learned no rain had been forecasted that day. I went upstairs and handed Carol her coffee. I said, "I prayed and told God I wanted rain and thunder today as a sign that provision was coming this year." She looked at me like I was crazy.

I was volunteering in the high school youth group at our church. I left church around 10:30. As I was driving down Glade Rd, I looked up at a clear blue sky. I said, "Well, God... I picked a good day to ask for rain and thunder, there's not even a cloud the size of a man's hand for you to work with." (See 1 Kings 18:44)

Around 2 p.m., I called my sister, who was living in Plymouth Mass. Her husband answered, and I asked him what he was doing. He said, "Well, I was watching the Colonial Golf tournament, but they postponed it." I said, "Because of thunder??" He said yes, and I told him I had to go. The Colonial is played in Fort Worth, roughly thirty-five miles from our home. I turned on the computer and pulled up the radar. There were four small storms around us. North, south, east, and west. The nearest storm was about twenty six miles north of us. I went out front and started pacing in my driveway, praying, pointing at the sky, rebuking anything and everything from interfering with the rain reaching me. My next-door neighbor came out to walk her dog and asked what I was doing. I said, "I'm waiting for rain and thunder." She looked up at a blue sky and said, "Oh, is it supposed to rain today??" I said, "I don't think so, but I told God I wanted rain and thunder today." She said, "Well, have a nice day." I have no idea what she thought, but that's what she said. I paced in and out of the house for probably two hours. I had never been here before. I was on the verge of a breakthrough, and nothing was going to get in the way of my prayer being answered. Around 4 pm, our oldest daughter asked if I'd take her to the health club. I told her I didn't know. I didn't want to leave and miss any rain at my house. I also didn't want to drive anywhere to get rained on. I had never been in this situation, and I didn't want to 'make' anything happen.

I agreed to take her and figured I would only be gone twenty minutes. We had to stop at her boyfriend's house (now husband) to pick something up. He only lived half a mile away. We got a quarter of a mile from our house when a single drop of rain hit the windshield. I put the window down and said, "THAT is not rain, that is a drop of water!" I said I wanted to get wet." When we pulled into his driveway, it was raining. The sun was shining, but it was raining. She got out of the car and ran inside. I got out of the car and stood on his front lawn. I raised both arms to the side and watched the rain hit my arms. I said, "Ok, I'm getting wet. Where's my thunder? I was very specific!" I called our youngest daughter, who was at home, and asked her if it was raining there. She said it was. Ok honey, thank you. I now know it's raining at my house. About thirty seconds later, I heard a distant rumble.

Excited, I called my daughter back and asked if she heard the thunder. She said no. Just then, there was a loud clap. I said, "Listen, listen!!" She said, "I heard it daddy" I started freaking out on their front lawn.

My daughter came out and said, "Dad!! Stop! You're making a scene!" I shouted, "NO!!... I WILL NOT STOP!! YOU DO NOT UNDERSTAND THE SIGNIFICANCE OF THIS DAY!! May 30, 2010 THE DAY YOUR FATHER PRAYED FOR RAIN AND THUNDER, AND GOD GAVE HIM RAIN AND THUNDER!! YOU WILL TELL YOUR CHILDREN OF THIS DAY!!" She said, "Can we just please leave?" We started driving towards the health club, and it started raining so hard that I could barely see to drive. Then it started hailing. I said, "It's hailing! I didn't ask for hail, but this is great!!" She said, "Hail is bad." I said, "No, this is good hail." We drove around two miles west, and the rain had stopped, and the sun was shining. The ground wasn't even wet.

She looked at me and asked, "Now, what did you pray for and why?" I went back home, and Carol arrived fifteen to twenty minutes later. She had tears in her eyes when she opened the door. She said, "I was in Walmart when I heard the thunder. When I walked outside, there was a rainbow. A rainbow signifies God's promise."

Friends who live a half mile from us told me it wasn't supposed to rain that day. They had watched the forecast and planned on painting their garage floor that day because no rain had been forecasted. They had taken everything out of the garage and were scrambling to put things back inside when it started. I said, "I'm sorry Judy, that was my fault." Also, our oldest son was in a brief holding pattern over DFW airport due to the storm.

In 1 Kings 17, Elijah told King Ahab there would be no dew or rain until Elijah prayed. God told Elijah to go east of Jordan to a valley with a brook. It also says God told ravens to bring him food both morning and night. Elijah stayed there for some time, then the brook dried up due to the lack of rain, which forced him to leave.

We find comfortable places in life and get used to the routine. I personally don't like change when things are going fine, but sometimes we are forced out of our comfort zones. The Lord told Elijah, "Go at once to Zarephath in the region of Sidon (modern day Syria) and stay there. I have directed a widow there to supply you with food." Because she was willing to give Elijah the first loaf of the last of her batch of bread, her flour and oil never ran out. Later, when the widow's son became sick and died, Elijah raised him from the dead. You may not believe that story is true, but I do. Jesus even mentioned it. *"I assure you that there were many widows in Israel in Elijah's time, when the sky was shut for three and a half years, and there was a severe famine throughout the land. Yet Elijah was not sent to any of them, but to a widow in Zarephath in the region of Sidon" Luke 4:25,26 NIV.* Why was Elijah sent to her and not one of the widows in Israel?

I didn't write the following analogy, but **I** have reflected on it countless times in the past twenty-five years. I've tried to find the author to give them credit, to no avail. I don't consider myself to be one of these people, but I will continue to try to become one.

Above The Timberline

Have you ever gone into the mountains high enough to see what is called a timberline? This is a certain height in elevation that varies according to locale, in which the trees do not grow anymore. Except for a few isolated or small groups of trees that survive in the higher elevation.

If you and I walk very close to Jesus, we will see some similarities between our lives and the trees that grow above the timberline. These trees are sometimes found clinging tenaciously to some rock cleft where the wind and elements of the weather lash unmercifully at the trees. Sometimes, little clusters give mutual support to one another from the rain, sleet, hail, and bitter cold. But unlike men or animals, the trees cannot shift to protect themselves from the harsh elements that come against them.

They usually are rooted in one spot and get tough or die. More often than not, these trees are not what we would call a 'perfect specimen' of the forest. To the onlooker, they can be distorted, bent, unbalanced, broken, or blasted by the elements. Branches can be torn and twisted from the trunk, caused by the elements of life. And yet some stick up in bold defiance against the storms of life. They do not enjoy the shelter of the ten thousand other trees in the forest, where life's cushy and less demanding. Instead, their life is one of living on the extreme edge of survival. Stress unequaled by their brothers and sisters of the forest.

These trees possess a unique beauty that can only be born of adversity. A beauty that comes only out of great agony and solitary suffering. They reflect a strength by standing against the stresses of life that those of the forest neither see nor understand.

In viewing these trees, we see a stirring example of the benefits of isolated adversity. These trees resemble rugged individuals, set apart from the common crowd. Having to stand alone in some remote spot against the rage of storms. Like us, rugged strength is not developed in the soft security of our peers. You and I will meet a few Christians who have withstood the isolation, hardships, and solitude of an extremely close walk with Jesus. But what a beauty, what a thrilling encounter it is to meet up with a man or woman of God like this.

There is an element to these trees that goes unnoticed by the casual observer. The type of wood produced in the lives of these trees is different from that of those in the forest. The extra stress and strain brought about by the adversity of the elements produce an extra flow of resins in the tree. This resin gives the tree a stronger fiber and a very tight-grained texture of wood. This enables it to stand alone. It also produces an exquisite fragrance that lower altitude trees cannot produce. But the wood, the very life of the tree, because of the extra resin, is more beautiful than any other wood.

It is sought after by expert violin makers because of its beauty over the other woods in the forest, and also because it has a musical resonance unequaled by that found in ordinary lumber. You see, the fury of the storms, the short growing season, the wrenching of the winds, the strain of isolated survival, are all factors combined to produce the toughest, choicest, most wonderful wood in the world. Is it possible that you've forgotten that you asked the Lord to make you into a "choice vessel?'

Some of us will endure privation and personal isolation. Some may have agonizing separation from those in the forest. But the beauty and richness that will come out of this type of life will last for all eternity. Don't fight the Lord if He has so chosen to plant you in an isolated spot. It will produce maturity and bring blessings that others from the forest will not get to experience.

God will give you the grace and strength to endure not shared with those in the forest. The view is another blessing that is obscured by those stuck in the forest. You'll see the approaching storms sooner (your brothers and sisters in the woods may think you're nuts), and you'll get glimpses of the Lord that the multitudes will never see. There will also be no crowding of others' roots for the choice nutrients or refreshing streams of water. If you are going to go very far in your walk, be assured that you will experience isolation. But only for a season. Don't let the dangers that encroach when isolation comes cause you to give up God's best for a second or third best. The dangers of self-pity, discontentment, loss of love, or losing sight of the eternal are things all of us face when we feel isolated and alone. God wants all of us to have his best.

But there's a price attached to it. Sometimes it's a life of isolation. Author Unknown

God Stories

Years ago, we were in Greece with a group of friends. When we were in Athens, I was just observing people as they walked by. I wasn't seeing any Christians. Sometimes I can tell when a person is a believer because I can see the Lord in their eyes. It's kind of odd, but it's true. Everyone was just rushing around doing their own thing. After Athens, we went to Samos, a small island just off the coast of Turkey. We had to pay a local fisherman named Yannis to take us to the Island of Patmos because the ferries had stopped the week before we arrived. It was an experience to say the least. On the trip back, we got into a fish fight with the crew of another fishing trawler that a friend of his owned.

Patmos is where John the Apostle wrote the Book of Revelation while he spent thirty years in exile there. I started seeing Christians everywhere!! I asked God why because there were so many. He said, "Where are you?" Patmos. "Why are you here?" It was a pilgrimage for me. There was a cruise ship in the harbor, and the people on it were there for the same reason I was.

A week after we arrived home, I went to a Christian business owners luncheon at Smokey's BBQ on Mockingbird Ln in Dallas that a friend suggested I attend. I didn't know anyone there. I had picked up a small baggie of gravelly sand from the shoreline on Patmos and felt prompted to bring it with me. There were around fifteen to twenty people in the room. The guest speaker got up to speak and said he was going to be speaking on John's exile on Patmos. A few minutes into his message, I raised my hand and asked if I could interrupt. A little annoyed, he said, "Well, that depends, what is it?" I told him I had just returned from Patmos and felt led to bring this bag of sand with me today. The room erupted. They asked me to pass it around. A few people asked if they could have some, which I agreed to.

I went to a seminar in Dallas in 2005. For privacy reasons, I won't mention who held the seminar, but you would recognise their names. One of the speakers had a New England accent. I went up to him after the group had finished speaking and I asked him where he was from in New England. He smiled and knew his accent had given him away. He grew up a few towns away from where I did. We had a little laugh. My next question was, "How long have you been a Christian?" Puzzled, he looked at me and asked, "How did you know I was a Christian?" I told him I could see the Lord in his eyes. He was shocked and started crying uncontrollably because he didn't feel like he still was. He pulled me aside and shared with me several things The Lord had done in his life.

Guilt, shame, and condemnation are powerful weapons the enemy will use against you.

Emotions make good servants, but horrible masters. Jesus said He would never leave or forsake us. We aren't worthy and can never make ourselves worthy. Forgiveness is a free gift. Ask Him for it.

There was a grapevine in the backyard of our second home when we bought it. Year after year, it only produced a few clusters of grapes but had thousands of leaves. It sprawled twenty feet plus each side of the vine. People walking by would comment on how beautiful it was. I thanked them, looked at it, and thought, but where's your fruit? The purpose of a grapevine is to produce fruit, not leaves.

In June 2004, I read the book "Secrets of the Vine" by Bruce Wilkerson. He and his wife had just bought a home in the country they'd always wanted. Separating his property from his neighbor, was a row of grapevines. He looked out one morning and, to his horror, saw his neighbor hacking away at it. He ran outside to introduce himself and hopefully get him to stop. Not sure of what to say, he said, "Don't like grapes??" The neighbor looked at him and said, "You must be from the city. I love grapes, it's the leaves that I don't like. You'll either have one or the other." As it turns out, my grapevine was putting all of its energy into producing leaves. It may have looked beautiful to the passerby, but its purpose was to produce fruit.

John 15 suddenly came alive!

"I am the true vine, and my Father is the gardener. He cuts off every branch in me that bears no fruit, while every branch that does bear fruit he prunes so that it will be even more fruitful. You are already clean because of the word I have spoken to you. Remain in me, as I also remain in you. No branch can bear fruit by itself; it must remain in the vine. Neither can you bear fruit unless you remain in me. "I am the vine; you are the branches. If you remain in me and I in you, you will bear much fruit; apart from me you can do nothing." John 15:1-5 NIV

I immediately went outside and started cutting away at my grapevine. When I had finished, I had two large piles of brush. I stood back and looked at the base of my vine and said, "Ok God, this is my life." I didn't know if it would even survive the shock of what I did to it. Nothing happened for seven days. It was then I saw my first new growth. From that point on, it exploded with growth. New flowering clusters of grapes were appearing on a daily basis. Within a month or so, I had over sixty clusters of grapes. It was a thirtyfold return from just one pruning!! I cut off the branches that didn't have any fruit. Within two months, I couldn't count the clusters of grapes! Grapevines will also produce more fruit than they can sweeten. Vineyards remove clusters before grapes are harvested. This increases the sugar content of the grapes left for harvest. (Brix level for wine is 20-28) The sugar content of grapes is checked daily just before harvest. I want to add that grapes are only produced from new branches each year. The branches from the previous year will NOT bear any fruit. Fruit trees also don't consume their own fruit. Likewise, our gifts and callings are not meant for our own consumption. Our fruit is intended to be a blessing to others. Be patient, it takes longer for fruit to ripen than it does for vegetables. *"But the fruit of the Spirit is love, joy, peace, patience, kindness, goodness, faithfulness, gentleness,   self-control. Against such things there is no law." Galatians 5:22,23 ESV*

One time, I had just dropped one of our daughters off at school, and three people cut me off one after the other. Each time I said, "Forgive them Lord, they know not what they do, and forgive them Lord, they're more important than me." I started thinking of everyone I've had to forgive over the years. I told God I was tired of always being the one who has to do the forgiving. I asked God, "Am I going to be doing this my whole life?" Immediately, He said, "Yes." I just started to laugh. Instantly, my attitude changed.

The circumstances didn't, but my attitude did. When we focus on ourselves, it usually goes downhill quickly and picks up speed.

I remember one Saturday morning when our oldest son was around fourteen. I was late and had to get to the restaurant to make bread. In the rush and stress to leave the house, I yelled at him about something. On my drive to work, God told me I needed to go back and apologize to him. I didn't have time. I was already late. He told me a second time. I turned around and went and told him I was sorry.

It changed my entire outlook and mood for that day. I don't remember that thirty minutes disruption to my schedule affecting my day at all. Could that have scarred my son in some way if I hadn't gone back? Resentment takes hold as a seed. Left alone, it will grow and take on a life of its own. Do not give the enemy any ground to establish a foothold.

If God should give your heart a check, you must not let it bounce

It's not a sacrifice of praise, but obedience that counts

I struggled with the following passage in Matthew for years. I used to pray that Jesus would never say this to me, *"Not everyone who says to me, 'Lord, Lord,' will enter the kingdom of heaven, but only the one who does the will of my Father who is in heaven. Many will say to me on that day, 'Lord, Lord, did we not prophesy in your name and in your name drive out demons and in your name perform many miracles?' Then I will tell them plainly, 'I never knew you. Away from me, you evildoers!' Matthew 7:21-23 NIV*

One day, while meditating on that passage and God saying that to me when I stood before Him. He asked me in that still small voice, "Could I say that to you?" I thought about it and said no, you do know me, and I know you. He said, "Then don't worry about it, it doesn't apply to you." If He said He never knew me, He'd be a liar. Truth will always bear witness with truth. Jesus said, He is The Way, The Truth, and The Life, and no one comes to the Father except through Him. He's not a way, He is The Way. Ask Him for yourself if you know Him and if He knows you. He will answer you.

I was at a tire store getting a used tire so my car would pass inspection. I looked to my left and saw an elderly woman there alone. She looked uncomfortable and out of place, so I walked over and struck up a conversation with her. She said she was at Walmart, and they said her tire was going to cost her a hundred dollars. She told them she didn't have a hundred dollars, and someone said she could get a used tire at this place for twenty dollars. I glanced down and noticed that she had holes in her shoes. Just then, God told me to buy her tire. I reminded Him I was buying a used tire myself so I could pass inspection, and I only had thirty dollars on me. Immediately He said, "You have a new Michelin spare you've never used. Ask them how much they'd charge you to put that on your rim." They told me ten dollars. I said ok, do that. I also want to buy that lady's tire. They finished her car before mine. She went to pay them, and the guy said, "No no, him pay already." She was shocked. She walked over to me and said, "You bought me a tire? Why did you do that??" I said, "Because God asked me to." She looked up to the sky with tears in her eyes and said, "Thank you." It was only twenty dollars, but it was all that I had.

It's not how much you give, but how much of you gives it.

I've wondered if she's told people about the time God bought her a tire. I can't take credit for it because it wasn't me. It wasn't even my idea.

We used to have a small prayer group at our home on Friday nights. We would take turns praying individually about what was on our hearts. I was asking God what I could do for Him to prove my love and commitment towards Him. I was thinking along the lines of traveling anywhere He wanted me to go, getting a bullhorn, standing on street corners, and sharing the Gospel.

I was willing to go, say, or do anything He asked me to. He answered me immediately and said, "Your daily life." That's all I ask. To seek and walk with Him daily, and to resist temptations that come. He reminded me that Jesus said, "It is finished." There's nothing we can do to add to what He's already done. Obedience is better than sacrifice.

There was a woman, Janie, whom we went to church with, but she always came alone. She was married, and her husband wasn't a believer.

I had purchased a new Thompson Chain Reference Bible from my uncle. He worked with a Christian school and got them for half price. It had a top-grain leather cover and even smelled wonderful. I went up to Janie before service started to show it to her. She looked at it and said how beautiful it was. When she did, God spoke to me and said, "Buy her one." Janie's Bible was the King James Version. I ordered one in top grain leather from my uncle. It arrived three weeks later. I brought it up and handed it to her before the service started. She flipped through it and said, "Oh brother, this is beautiful." I said, "I'm glad you like it, it's yours." She was shocked and started to cry.

She said she had prayed that morning that if she received her allowance from her husband on Monday, she would use it to buy a new Bible for herself because hers was falling apart. That's when I told her I had ordered it three weeks before she even asked. God is good. I have no idea if the next two stories are fact or fiction. I just like them for the lessons they teach.

There's a story of two pastors walking down a path, going fishing. The younger one, fresh out of seminary, asked the older one, "What is something you could tell me teach me that would give me a powerful, effective ministry?" The older pastor thought about it and said, "There's nothing I could tell you that would give you that." The young man was very disappointed. As they were fly fishing, the older pastor jumped on the younger pastor's shoulders, forcing him underwater. The young pastor was amused and figured he'd play along. When he needed to take a breath, he tried to surface, but the older pastor wouldn't let him up. He started fighting with all he had, but to no avail. He thought, "This guy is crazy! He's going to drown me!" About the time he was ready to take in water, the older pastor pulled him up. The young man looked at the old pastor like he was crazy as he gasped for breath. The older pastor looked intensely at him and said, "When you want to hear from God as bad as you wanted that breath of air, you'll have a powerful, effective ministry."

Years ago, I heard a story of a homeless man who was seeking God. He went to a large church downtown and tried to enter. He was turned away at the door because of his appearance. He walked to the curb, sat down, and started sobbing, thinking God had rejected him. Jesus appeared to him and asked him why he was crying. He looked up and said, They wouldn't let me in your house. Jesus replied, That's not my house, I've been trying to get in there for thirty years.

Just as I Am

Never think or believe you have no value, nothing to offer, or that God can't use you. Remember, Peter had a temper, David had an affair and tried to cover it up with murder, Noah had a drinking problem, Jonah ran from God, Paul was a murderer, Jacob was a cheater, Rahab and Mary Magdalene were prostitutes, Martha worried about everything, Thomas was a doubter, Sarah was impatient, Elijah was moody, Moses stuttered and also killed a man, Abraham was old, and Lazarus was dead. God doesn't call the qualified, He qualifies the called.

This is a precious story I recently read about a woman who believed she had nothing to bring to God. On September 22, 1871, an elderly British lady, 82 years young, was ushered into her heavenly reward. Earlier in her life, in 1835, her frustration at being an invalid left her feeling useless and questioning her very salvation. What she did next would echo through history.

As a young woman, Charlotte Elliot was not sure of her relationship with Christ, not sure of how to be saved, even though she had been raised a minister's daughter. The probing question of a Swiss evangelist, "Are you at peace with God?" would not leave her mind. When she saw the evangelist a few weeks later, she mentioned that she could not shake his question.

But, she protested, what could she possibly bring to God? When he replied that she need not bring anything but herself, she gladly accepted Christ. Some twelve years later, in 1835, crippled by illness and constant fatigue, she felt saddened by her inability to help a local church's cause. Remembering her conversion, she took out pen and paper and wrote a poem to encourage others who felt perhaps they too had nothing to give.

"Just As I Am, without one plea, But that Thy blood was shed for me,

And that Thou bidst me come to Thee, Oh, Lamb of God, I come..."

Her poem was published, and she was inundated with requests for it. She was glad to discover later that some copies were being sold to raise money for the very cause she felt helpless to assist. After her death, thousands of letters were found in her home, written by people whose lives had been transformed by her words. Her song has been translated into hundreds of languages, published in more than sixteen hundred hymnals, and has reached billions around the world, and continues to bring people to Christ even today.

Sixty years later, on this date, in 1931, a thirty-one-year old man riding in the sidecar of his brother's motorcycle in England finally came to the end of his internal struggle against whether Christ was indeed the Son of God. He finally knew in his soul that indeed Jesus was just who He said He was! He realized that God calls us to Him "just as we are". When C.S. Lewis stepped out of the sidecar, he was a new man, saved by grace! Ninety-nine years after Charlotte Elliott penned her words, and three years after Lewis' conversion, the sixteen-year-old son of a dairy farmer listened intently as he heard the message of salvation preached at a revival service in Charlotte, NC. When the song, "Just As I Am," was sung at the end, young Billy Graham went forward to accept Christ. Twenty years later, Billy Graham had become a successful evangelist and was invited to speak at Cambridge University in England. His nervousness over the event nearly led him to cancel it. But he was introduced to a kind man named C.S. Lewis, who encouraged him to disregard the critics who had spoken out against him, and to continue with the revival.

Rev. Graham went on to speak to an overflow crowd of two thousand each night of the revival, and when he returned to England in 1989, he addressed a crowd of eighty thousand at England's Wembley Stadium! As always, he closed the event with the same song that brought him to Christ, "Just As I Am." Never think you have nothing to bring to Jesus!

That is exactly what He wants you to bring... nothing! He wants you, just you, as you are! He can take frustration like Charlotte Elliot's, skepticism like Lewis', and nervousness like Billy Graham's, and reach the world through you! **"Just as I am, though tossed about, with many a conflict, many a doubt, fightings and fears within, without, O Lamb of God, I come, I come."**

Some of my favorite quotes

P reach The Gospel at all times and if necessary use words." **Attributed to St Francis of Asisi**

"You wouldn't worry so much about what others think of you if you realized how seldom they do." **Eleanor Roosevelt**

"If you never heal from what hurt you... you'll bleed on those that didn't cut you." **Pastor Craig Lemley**

Love is patient, love is kind. It does not envy, it does not boast, it is not proud. It does not dishonor others, it is not self-seeking, it is not easily angered, it keeps no record of wrongs. Love does not delight in evil but rejoices with the truth. It always protects, always trusts, always hopes, always perseveres. 1 Corinthians 13:3-8 NIV

"Some of the wise will stumble, so that they may be refined, purified and made spotless until the time of the end, for it will still come at the appointed time." Daniel 11:35 NIV

"If you do not stand firm in your faith, you will not stand at all." Isaiah 7:9 NIV

Trust in the Lord with all your heart, and lean not on your own understanding. In all your ways acknowledge Him, and He shall direct your paths. Proverbs 3:5,6 NKJV

Do not look where you fell, but where you slipped **African Proverb**

Friends are made by many acts and lost by only one. **Harvey Mackey**

"Some days, the grace of God allows you to enjoy what is happening, other days, the grace of God allows you to endure what is happening." **Unknown**

"God allows in His wisdom what He could easily prevent by His power." **Graham Cooke**

"Think how you have instructed many, how you have strengthened feeble hands. Your words have supported those who stumbled; you have strengthened faltering knees. " Job 4: 3,4 NIV

"But if you harbor bitter envy and selfish ambition in your hearts, do not boast about it or deny the truth. For where you have envy and selfish ambition, there you find disorder and every evil practice. " James 3:14,16 NIV

One moment of patience may ward off great disaster. One moment of impatience may ruin a whole life. **Chinese Proverb**

I'm very open-minded, I just have screens on my windows to keep the bugs out. **Myself**

You may be wise beyond your years, but still, your years are few.   Consider all you've learned till now, then multiply by two

You can't replace experience, life lessons will take time.

Time is what separates mere grape juice and fine wine. **Myself**

Sin will take you further than you wanted to go, keep you longer than you want to stay, and cost you more than you are willing to pay. **Author unknown**

"Alexander, Caesar, Charlemagne, and I myself have founded great empires; but upon what did these creations of our genius depend? Upon force. Jesus alone founded His empire upon love, and to this very day millions will die for Him." **Napoleon Bonaparte**

"I think I understand something of human nature, and I tell you, all these were men, and I am a man; none else is like Him: Jesus Christ was more than a man." **Napoleon Bonaparte**

"Christ alone has succeeded in so raising the mind of man toward the unseen, that it becomes insensible to the barriers of time and space. Across the chasm of eighteen hundred years, Jesus Christ makes a demand beyond all others difficult to satisfy; He asks for that which a philosopher may often seek in vain at the hands of his friends, or a father of his children, or a bride of her spouse, or a man of his brother. He asks for the human heart; He will have it entirely to Himself. He demands it unconditionally, and forthwith His demand is granted. Wonderful!

In defiance of time and space, the soul of man, with all its powers and faculties, becomes an annexation to the empire of Christ. All who sincerely believe in Him, experience that remarkable supernatural love towards Him. This phenomenon is unaccountable it is altogether beyond the scope of man's creative powers. Time, the great destroyer, is powerless to extinguish this sacred flame; time can neither exhaust its strength nor put a limit to its range. This is it, which strikes me most; I have often thought of it. This is it, which proves to me quite convincingly the Divinity of Jesus Christ." **Napoleon Bonaparte**

About the cover

The disciple Nathanael was my inspiration for the cover. *Philip found Nathanael and told him, "We have found the one Moses wrote about in the Law, and about whom the prophets also wrote—Jesus of Nazareth, the son of Joseph."*

"Nazareth! Can anything good come from there?"

Nathanael asked. "Come and see," said Philip. When Jesus saw Nathanael approaching, he said of him, "Here truly is an Israelite in whom there is no deceit." "How do you know me?" Nathanael asked. Jesus answered, "I saw you while you were still under the fig tree before Philip called you." John 1:45-48 NIV